THE SPIDER:
REIGN OF THE SILVER TERROR

THE SPIDER

MASTER OF MEN! ®

REIGN OF
THE SILVER TERROR

By Grant Stockbridge

ALTUS PRESS • 2019

CHAPTER 1
DEATH BELOW

A WHISPER of sound jerked Wentworth's eyes upward to the mouth of the mine shaft. A choked cry tore from his throat. He flung himself frantically to the left, clinging by his hands alone to one side of the ladder.

A huge boulder was tumbling down the shaft! So large it blotted out daylight, the boulder hurtled downward with express-train speed, rushing straight at Wentworth!

If it struck him, he would be crushed to a pulp. Even if it missed, the whistling suction of its passage might snatch him from his precarious hold, plunge him to shattering death at the bottom of the shaft.

These thoughts were a flash in Wentworth's brain. In the instant before the boulder had toppled into the shaft, he glimpsed a man's head against the spot of daylight at the top. He knew this was a deliberate attempt at murder, a part of the country-wide plot he had come to this mine to block.

Wentworth's lips were locked grimly, his eyes molten with rage as, peering upward from where he clung to the ladder, he sought to estimate the size of the falling rock, to gauge his chances of escape. The boulder had only three hundred feet to fall from the top, a matter of moments. But those fleet instants must be enough. If the Spider died here, there would be no one

to warn the unsuspecting nation, no one to rescue it from the clutches of this criminal band.

Wentworth drew his knees upward, braced his feet firmly against the side of the ladder, jammed his shoulders against

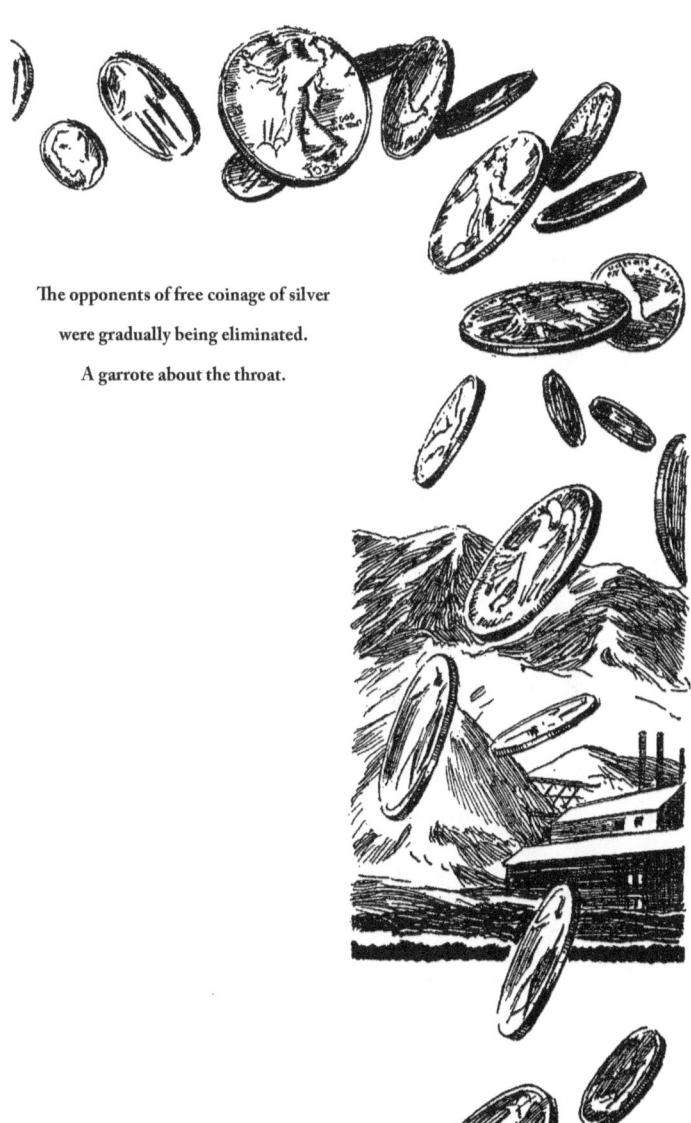

The opponents of free coinage of silver
were gradually being eliminated.
A garrote about the throat.

the side wall of the shaft. He loosened his hand-hold, seized a wall-brace above his head. He was clear of the ladder now, flat against the wall of the shaft. He could only wait.

A hot belch of air gushed at him. The boulder brushed the ladder above. It quivered violently and Wentworth's feet were shaken from its side. He dangled by his hands alone, clinging with arms thrown backward above his head, interlacing ringers locked about a brace. Straight at him, the jagged chunk of ore rushed!

One of its jutting points crunched against the wall not fifteen feet above his head. The point smashed off. Stone ground harshly on stone. Fragments hailed on Wentworth. Half-dazed by the battering of the rock splinters, he flattened himself helplessly, nervously, against the wall. In an instant….

The boulder was past! So close that a whirling point bruised his thigh, the huge block of ore swished past. That jarring bounce against the wall had saved him! Wentworth's arms were numb from the jerk of that glancing blow. Half-stunned by the pounding rocky fragments, he cumbersomely raised his feet, groped for the ladder. In a moment the pulling suction of the rock's passage….

He curled his toes above a round of the ladder and a fury of winds tore at him. They whined and roared through the shaft, whipped his clothing, snatched his hat from his head and spun it downward into blackness.

Wentworth's arms and legs ached with clinging. He raised his voice in a wild despairing cry, a shriek that dwindled weakly, was chopped off short when the rock crashed to the bottom and sent its fearful echoes slapping up the shaft.

For moments longer, Wentworth clung with toes and hands to his hold, then with tedious caution, he loosed one foot and planted it against the side of the ladder. When the pressure held his shoulders securely against the wall, he released the other foot and braced it beneath the other, strained his arms forward.

A faint, grim smile on his lips, Wentworth swung himself to the rounds of the ladder and clung there, peering cold-eyed up toward the head of the shaft. Perhaps he had fooled that man up there with his scream which had simulated the cry of a person falling to death. Perhaps he had, but Wentworth doubted it. He had pretended to be a friend of Harry Black, the owner of this mine; he had said he wished to descend by the ladder to surprise Black. The guard had seemed to agree—then, when the Spider was three hundred feet down, this boulder had toppled down the shaft! The man above, it seemed, was not credulous.

WENTWORTH KNEW definitely now that Harry Black was warned of his coming—Black who seemed to be involved in the vast silver conspiracy which already had cost two lives, which threatened now to cost the Spider's too. His grim smile tightened his lips away from his teeth, Wentworth touched the automatic in the clip beneath his left arm. He was ready for further attacks.

Slowly, hand under hand, he continued the descent. He knew the geography of the Silver Lode mine pretty well. It was a modified glory-hole construction. That is, the ore was hauled out at the lowest level through a nearly horizontal passageway that opened on the side of the mountain. There was a main shaft which met this at a vertical right angle. In the usual glory-hole, this shaft would be enlarged gradually from the surface and the ore would be dumped down the shaft as down a chute. Black had varied this plan and run levels off from the shaft, but ore was dumped downward to be hauled out.

For that reason, there was no cage in the main shaft except a hand-power winch for lowering tools. Men used the ladder. It was laborious, reaching Black from above this way, but Wentworth had chosen it deliberately in order to approach unobserved.

He paused abruptly, listening. Just below, he caught the slow squeak of a turning wheel. His keen eyes pierced the darkness, made out a dim glimmer of light, saw a wheelbarrow load of ore dumped into the shaft. It rattled downward, the wheel squeaked, the light dwindled. This was the fourth level he had passed. Three more down, and he would reach the cut where Black was supervising the setting of some blasts.

Wentworth waited until no more sounds came from the black opening in the sides of the shaft. Then he continued his slow descent. He must pass in silence or the death he momentarily expected might spit from that blackness! Distantly a bell raised dim clangor. Wentworth's eyes narrowed. That would be the mine phone system; that would be the man on the surface warning Black! Now, indeed, death would stalk his footsteps.

Wentworth eased on downward, watching, listening. Wentworth had flown to Denver after Senator Racktat, one of the major opponents of free coinage of silver, had been murdered in a Washington hotel. A strangler had thrown a garrote about his throat from behind, snapped his vertebrae with a quick wrench. The Spider's voluminous clipping service had informed him that a man had been strangled in Denver in the same way. That man had been paymaster for a silver mine and he was robbed of four thousand dollars.

When Wentworth reached Denver, following the trail of the stranglers, he learned from the police that some of this four thousand dollars, identified by serial numbers, had turned up in a jewelry store and had, apparently, been spent by Harry Black.

So Wentworth, envisioning on the basis of his private information the beginnings of another of those titanic plots against the people which the Spider alone could combat successfully, had come for Black. He used forged credentials from Washington to delay police action and reach his man unheralded.

And now, closing in on his suspect, Wentworth found additional confirmation of his fears in these attempts upon his life. In Washington, he had watched with increasing concern the growth of a lobby for free silver. One after another, leading Congressmen and Senators opposed to free silver had been silenced. They had ceased to oppose the measures and some even had spoken in favor of the bills, professing themselves convinced by arguments. The Spider had learned what those arguments were. Blackmail! Extortion! Bribery!

Senator Shokum's past had yielded a lever to move him; Congressman Whinkle's daughter had been kidnapped—her ransom, her father's silence; Senator Fulcrim had accepted a ten thousand dollar equity in a silver mine; these were "facts, Wentworth knew, but it was not possible to prove them.

On top of these crimes had come the murder of Senator Racktat!

There was no longer any doubt that an unscrupulous agency was at work, seeking to sway the nation's legislation, and Wentworth plunged heart and soul into the battle. It was not that he was fighting silver legislation because of his own personal belief that it was harmful, it was not that he doubted the sincerity of many of the free silver advocates; it was simply that the methods were criminal.

WENTWORTH, WITH his deep knowledge of underworld psychology, realized the menacing potentialities of a group which gained sufficient power to control the national legislature. Power-drunk, they might drive the nation again to the brink of financial ruin, they might completely debase the currency for their own selfish ends. Wentworth saw versions of tottering closing banks, of long hopeless lines of depositors, of privation and riots—the old toll of depression.

But the malevolent powers concealed themselves well. Nowhere in the east could Wentworth gain any clue to the men behind this criminal flood. The lobby itself he was familiar with, but it was almost inconceivable that they should join forces with these murderers. Ram Singh, his Hindu body servant, was checking that faint possibility even now. So Wentworth had dropped his fruitless Washington investigations and flown west, hoping to uncover some lead.

It seemed he might succeed. Apparently one of the Silver

Assassins' minions has slipped outside the fold for a little private practice in that holdup—and the Spider was on his trail!

Wentworth halted and flashed a minute beam of light from a pocket torch. He had reached the level where the suspect, Harry Black, was working. The level where murder must lurk. No one, no movement, was visible. The Spider switched off the light, made his way warily into the mouth of the tunnel and stood, listening tensely in the blackness.

Distantly he could distinguish the metallic clatter of drills. Behind him, in the shaft, another barrow-load of ore rattled downward. These were the only sounds, yet Wentworth was sure the man above had phoned a warning, was sure that somewhere here murder awaited him. He opened his mouth wide to breath. Even a quick nasal inhalation would be noisy within these crowding walls. The air was hot and close. He felt perspiration run slow, cold threads down his sides.

Black would be warned, but he would not know that it was the Spider who came for him. Had he known that, he might have fled screaming from the mine. All the world feared the vengeance of that grim nemesis of criminals who called himself the Spider. Long ago, Wentworth had sworn to become the scourge of the underworld, long ago when he had realized how futile were the attempts of police to overpower the master minds of crime who periodically flung their cohorts against civilization.

Police did excellent work with the routine suppression of criminals but against the ingenious designs of master criminals they were powerless. So the Spider had been born—so he carried on his ceaseless crusade of justice.

Wentworth thought of these things as, satisfied no one lurked behind him, he pushed soft-footed into the bowels of the earth, following a trail of silver and death, knowing that at any moment the blackness might split with the red flame of a murder shot.

Sharply, the Spider halted his advance. Had that been a footfall just ahead? He thrust his flashlight far out to one side, squeezed the button. The thin beam darted into the blackness. Suddenly, Wentworth dropped the light, lunged forward in a violent, head-long dive.

His light had revealed a crouched man in the middle of the passageway with a miner's sharp, short-handled pick poised to strike! At the spark of light, he had sprung forward, swinging the pick viciously downward!

IN THE instant the man swept his murderous pick downward, Wentworth's shoulder slammed against his stomach, sent him reeling backward. They pitched down together. Wentworth heard the pick clatter on the rack floor behind him. His hands closed on the man's throat. He gouged forefingers beneath the ears, seeking the nerve centers that would paralyze instantly.

In the back of the Spider's mind an alarm rang. Many times before this he had battled in the dark, many times before had felt a man's throat cords slide beneath his fingers. He knew that a man may fight such a hold two ways. He may fight the wrists that strangle him, or he may reach for another weapon. The hands of the man he throttled did not touch Wentworth's body, nor did they seek to break his hold. It was a danger signal! The Spider did not loosen his hold, but with a thrust of his legs hurled himself forward in a somersault over the man's head. As he shot through the air, he felt a ripping tug at his breeches and knew that he had missed by less than a heartbeat the burning stab of a knife in his vitals!

In his dive, Wentworth had not let go his hold. His shoulder struck the floor while his fingers still gripped the man's throat. As his roll continued, his hips swinging downward, he tensed his arms and threw all his strength and the weight of his fall into a wrenching heave on the assassin's neck.

The man's body jerked upward then Wentworth's fingers tore loose. He continued his somersault and rolled smoothly to his feet. Instantly he whirled, crouched alertly, balanced on his toes.

He heard the man's breath, hoarse and horrible in his throat. Two, three, four times the rattling exhalations turned the black tunnel into a nightmare pit. The fifth breath hesitated, then came out in an expiring groan. After that was silence.

Wentworth, a hard smile on his lips, slipped a cigarette lighter from his pocket and snapped it to flame. The man lay motionless on his back, neck twisted unnaturally, broken by the Spider's shrewd wrench. A knife was clenched in his right hand. One more murderer had gone to his punishment.

Wentworth stooped for a moment over the corpse, setting the base of the cigarette lighter upon its forehead. The quivering flame threw grotesque shadows on the in-crowding walls, showed the Spider crouching above his kill, a tall man of smooth strength clad in a flannel shirt and riding breeches.

He was in disguise, his face narrow and gaunt with skillful shadowing, his nose thin and hawk-like; but there was a hard glitter in the gray-blue eyes that looked down upon his prey; a

11

small tight smile upon the lips that betrayed the man beneath this mask. This was Richard Wentworth, scion of wealth who gave his life so that others might have the peace and happiness he must ever deny himself, who stepped thus outside the law so that the law might be made stronger. Actually, the greatest benefactor of humanity in the modern world, legally he was a criminal and a murderer, hounded by the police of a hundred nations.

But Wentworth laughed at the police he assisted so ably— and who of necessity repaid him with persecution. For the law cannot consider the motives of the man who kills. Clear-eyed, Wentworth had realized these facts before the Spider had been born. Deliberately he had made the sacrifice that humanity might be shielded.

As Wentworth straightened from beside the body of the assassin, as he lifted the lighter, there glimmered on the paling flesh of the dead man's brow a sinister emblem, a small spot of blood-red that had sprawling, hairy legs. It was the seal of the Spider, the calling card of death that he left behind to warn criminals to abandon their evil ways lest they, too, fall beneath his fatal brand!

When he had imprinted the seal, Wentworth recovered his flashlight, dragged the man's body to the brink of the shaft and tumbled it downward. Then he pushed on. Harry Black, who had sent the killer would expect his return. Wentworth could advance openly now. He sent the thin beam of his light ahead. It glinted on rough walls, on pillars of ore left at intervals to support the roof. The pillars were streaked with the blue-black of silver. Now and then a bit of free metal glinted.

12

The sweat was pouring down Wentworth's face. Black used no forced ventilation in his mine, depending on those two entrances below and above to maintain circulation of air. For that reason the drive he followed would not be deep. The metallic clanking of the drills, the dull heavy blows of sledges already were much louder. Wentworth frowned. Black used the cheapest of methods. No pneumatic drills, no cage, no ventilation system—yet he installed telephones! Wentworth shook his head. It was a strange combination.

AHEAD HE made out the glimmer of lights. He switched off his own flash and ducked through a low opening into a small chamber where four men worked at drills while a fifth stood watching. An oil lantern, hung from the handle of a pick, spread smoky, yellow light.

Wentworth touched the gun under his arm and once more a tight smile played across his lips. "Harry Black," he said, "may I speak with you?" His voice was deep, deeper even than Wentworth's normal tones, and the words boomed in the small chamber.

The man who stood watching jerked as if struck and whirled with arms tense. The four workmen looked up, startled. "Who are you?" Black demanded harshly. "How did you get here?"

His face was shadowed by the lantern's flicker, but Wentworth saw that his shoulders were broad as his own; that his six-foot height matched his, too. He saw also that the man's curly hair began high up on his brows, leaving a sweep of forehead that was strong and intelligent.

"I am a government agent," Wentworth said slowly. "I want

to talk with you." He intended to crash into this man's mind the fact that his assassin was dead, but at the last moment he changed his mind.

The stiff aggressiveness went out of Black's manner instantly, but there was still anger in the poise of his head, in the abruptness with which he turned back to the men.

"Go ahead with the drilling," he said brusquely, "but don't set the charges until I come back." He stepped close to where dynamite holes were being drilled. Wentworth saw that he intended to blast a huge block of ore from overhead down into the chamber. Black pointed out where to drill three more holes, then turned to Wentworth.

"If you had phoned," he said shortly, "I'd have been glad to come to you. I don't allow strangers in the mine." He stepped aside for Wentworth to duck first out of the chamber, drew a long-barreled flashlight from his belt and sent its circle dancing ahead of them. It seemed necessary to force the darkness back, as if it were a crouching enemy that retreated reluctantly before a superior force. To Wentworth, it was strangely ominous.

Black clumped silently along for half the distance to the shaft, staring moodily at the stubborn blackness, the glint of seepage-stained rock. Then he spoke abruptly, his voice sharp with a slight hurried, impatient enunciation as if words were too slow a vehicle for his thoughts.

"Lot of trouble here recently. Explosions, cave-ins, floods."

He glanced suddenly at Wentworth. "That's why I asked the government to investigate."

Wentworth's blue-gray gaze narrowed. This man did not talk like a criminal. Nor did criminals send for government agents. The fact that Black had asked for investigation meant that danger hung like a sword over the Spider's head. Wentworth had told police in Denver that he was a government agent. At any time the real government agent might visit the police—and would reveal immediately that Wentworth was an impostor. If, acting on that knowledge, they found that Spider-branded corpse in the shaft... Wentworth jerked his shoulders in an impatient shrug.

As usual peril stalked his heels. He must be prepared. He shot a side-glance at the man walking beside him. Black's profile, clear-cut against the back-glow of his flash, was intelligent, confirming the Spider's first estimate of that sweeping forehead. The jaw was long and lean and just now clamped hard. Black was frowning.

A new thought occurred to Wentworth. Why, if Black had sent for a government agent, had two of his men attempted to murder the Spider? They hadn't known Wentworth's identity, of course, but such actions hinted at guilt. He peered warily at Black.

Suddenly, without warning, an overwhelming gust of air struck their backs, hurled them face down in the tunnel. A violent, rumbling concussion rolled over them.

CHAPTER 2
"THE SPIDER!"

THE ROCK floor trembled beneath Wentworth and the acrid bite of dynamite fumes gnawed at his nostrils. He sprang to his feet. Black's light blazed again in the smoky darkness and the mine owner reeled up from the floor, whirled and plunged back the way he had come.

"Come back," Wentworth snapped. "Those fumes!"

Black's light already was twenty feet ahead of him. Outlined against it, the man's body was doubled forward at the waist. He was running. Abruptly he stumbled, reeled against the wall. He crumpled to his knees. Wentworth cursed. He bound a handkerchief over nose and mouth. Breathing lightly, he darted to Black's side, heaved the almost unconscious man to his shoulder and raced for the shaft.

Despite the handkerchief, the fumes were biting into his lungs. He thrust the light into his belt, crowded the bend of his elbow tight against his face and fought on. Finally, the swifter movement of thick smoke that fogged the passage told him the shaft was near. The draft was sucking it downward. He reached the chamber beside the shaft, dropped Black, rolled him over on his face to take advantage of the dearer air near the floor.

The miner was not unconscious. His arms and legs still moved weakly.

"Get out of here. Get masks," he mumbled.

He crawled fumblingly toward the shaft, pulled a phone from a rocky niche. Wentworth suddenly understood why the system

16

had been installed while other modern equipment had been neglected. Black had hinted at sabotage just before the blast. The phone was to protect the men.

It was ten minutes before a rescue crew arrived with masks, twenty more before they had hauled out the two men who, alive but gravely injured, could he extricated from that bell chamber within. The other two drillers had been killed instantly by the explosion. Black believed a charge of dynamite had been planted in a masked hole and touched off by a drill.

On the surface again, he faced Wentworth with a face on which rage sat blackly. "That is the sort of—thing I was talking about," he said hoarsely. "It's happening all about here. This is the third time it has struck me."

He gestured toward a rude cabin built against the side of the mountain and Wentworth strode beside him. His mind was combing over other information which he had gleaned from his newspaper clippings, information which previous to this he had not connected with the criminal activities of the Washington killers. He remembered that there had been a series of disasters in silver mines in Colorado and Nevada.

In a famous old shaft near Virginia City, a long-dammed underground riser had burst loose and drowned a score of men; there had been explosions and three or four cave-ins with heavy loss of life.

Wentworth's lips grew as thin as Black's. The menace was even greater than he had thought. Not alone were the criminals working to force through legislation which would favor their cause, but they were operating, apparently, against rivals in the mining field, determined to reap alone the rewards of their infamy.

But why, if these mine disasters were the work of a gang, did one occur in the mine of a man to whom the evidence pointed as at least a collaborator in the conspiracy? That terrific underground explosion with its pitiful toll of dead and injured had for the moment driven from Wentworth's mind the fact that evidence connected this man with the garrote hold-up murder which had brought him West.

Black stepped aside as they reached the cabin. Wentworth proceeded him warily, alert for an attack. Just inside the door, he stopped. There were two other persons in the cabin. A man and a woman rose from chairs at a desk. Both wore riding clothes, the girl was in jodhpurs and her blouse of white silk showed the youthful column of her throat.

"We phoned to Leadville—for a doctor, Harry," the girl said. Her voice was a deep contralto. It throbbed with anger.

Black nodded slowly. "Thanks, Bessie," he said. "Didn't know you were here, Tony."

The man was sturdily built, shorter than Wentworth, but with massive shoulders and chest that spoke of great strength and endurance. "By God, Harry," he stormed, "how much longer are you going to remain quiet? How much longer are you going to submit to murder and sabotage?"

His tones were slightly oratorical. Wentworth examined him beneath half-lowered lids. The man's face was dark, massive as his bodily build, with a square-set determined jaw blued by a close-shaven beard. His hair was thick and curly. He seemed sincere despite the forensic periods.

"Is this another agent of the syndicate?" he demanded, glaring at Wentworth, his heavy shoulders rolling forward.

"This is a government agent," Harry Black said quietly, and the words brought a twinge of remembrance to Wentworth. The real government agent was on his way here. At any moment he might arrive with police! "He was in the mine with me when the dynamite let go," Black went on. "That was a plant, Tony. Somebody deliberately—"his voice broke hoarsely. "Somebody deliberately murdered my men!"

"Somebody!" jeered the man called Tony. "Somebody! The whole state knows who that somebody is. It's the Syndicate! It's Roscoe Sinclair!"

BLACK SHRUGGED and turned to Wentworth. "I forget your name," he said. Wentworth told him "Haggard" and Black made the introductions.

"Bessie Kendall, my fiancée," he gestured toward the girl. Wentworth nodded curtly, then stepped forward as the girl offered her hand. Her clasp was cool and friendly, like her level blue eyes. There was a healthy color in her cheeks and her hair was a honey-golden brown. Nothing fragile about her. She would be steadfast, Wentworth thought, smiling at her, and she would have strength to endure, courage to fight.

"And this is Tony Sinclair," said Black.

Wentworth faced the belligerent glare of the broad-shoul-dered man, felt his hand gripped strongly. "Comrade Sinclair,"

the man said, still with that slight verbal flourish as if he stood upon a platform.

Wentworth's eyes met his dark stare steadily. "Not by any chance related to the Roscoe Sinclair you're blaming?" he asked. "Come to think of it, you're much the same build."

Tony Sinclair stepped back. "He's my father, blast his soul to hell! Foster father, he calls it, but I know better. He adopted me after his neglect killed my mother. But he can't buy me off

ROSCOE SINCLAIR

BESSIE KENDALL

HARRY BLACK

like that." He choked himself off abruptly. "That's all beside the point," he said gruffly. "Roscoe Sinclair and his syndicate did it."

Facts were assembling themselves in Wentworth's mind. Tony Sinclair was a radical agitator, a leader in the communist miner's union. There had been newspaper magazine spreads on his leaving his foster-father's house to join the Communists.

He had even defied the threat of disinheritance to work for "the Revolution." The reason for all that was clear now. Young Sinclair had discovered his supposed foster-father's betrayal of his mother and Tony's love for her—his hatred of the man who had wrecked her life—had grown into a hatred of the entire capitalistic class.

Wentworth turned to Black. "Is there any proof that the syndicate or Sinclair is behind these mine disasters?" he asked. He must work fast. That government agent and police might come at any moment. The Spider must be gone before then.

Black was frowning at the floor. He looked up at Wentworth, jerked a hand in an indefinite gesture. "Nothing definite," he said.

"Nothing definite!" Tony Sinclair roared. His voice made the windows vibrate.

Wentworth turned toward him impatiently. "Stop making speeches," he snapped. "If you've got proof, spill it."

The man swelled until his massive chest threatened to burst buttons from his gray flannel shirt. Muscles writhed in his hairy forearms. Wentworth turned his back on him. He was deliberately goading the agitator, seeking to force swift, truthful talk. He must hurry. He waited for the explosion from Sinclair. It didn't come. When he did speak, it was calmly. "You're quite right," he said quietly. "But I find it hard to keep calm on the subject."

Wentworth turned to the man with a new respect.

"There is no definite proof," Sinclair went on. "The syndicate has been trying to buy Harry out. He's got damned little money to operate on and an explosion such as today's will just about ruin him. It means that he will practically be forced to sell out! That's the proof, all there is of it."

"I won't sell," Black said stubbornly.

"Don't let them make you," Bessie Kendall urged. She went past Wentworth toward Harry Black.

Wentworth frowned. Black was hard up. Certain stolen money had passed through his hands. All the circumstances might have been framed—even that explosion below—as cover for criminal operations if the man were shrewd enough. He studied Black's face as he stood gazing unsmilingly down at his fiancée. Black seldom smiled. The man was intelligent all right smart enough for such a trick. And there was no explanation yet of those murderous attacks upon Wentworth.

A sharp blow on the cabin door jerked Wentworth's eyes that way. Instantly he was in motion. He sprang behind the door as it swung violently inward. He knew it was the police. Already they had been informed that he was an impostor. Even if they didn't know of that body in the mine with its crimson Spider seal, his capture now would be fatal to his plans. It was more important than ever that he remain free to fight this direful combination which was corrupting Washington and despoiling the mines.

Crouched behind the door, Wentworth saw a long-barreled revolver leveled through the opening, glimpsed a leather-faced man with a deputy's star on his coat. Black had put Bessie Kendall aside and stood with his head thrust forward, glaring at the man. Neither Bessie nor Tony Sinclair moved.

"Black," the leather-faced deputy said, tight-voiced, "You're under arrest for murder!"

Black's shoulders swelled, his fists knotted at his sides. "Damned fool!" he said tensely, in his hurried, clipped speech. "Think I'd kill my own men? Wreck the mine?"

Sinclair took a half step forward, and the deputy's revolver pivoted to cover his broad chest.

"It's more of the filthy plotting of the syndicate!" he declaimed. "Is there no end to their infamy? Is there no limit…?"

"Pipe down, pipe down," growled the deputy. "This ain't got nothing to do with the mine explosion. Black's under arrest for killing that pay-master in Denver last week."

Wentworth placed his hand against the door. He knew what that meant. Police had discovered his imposture and decided to act at once against Black.

"That's asinine," Black snapped.

"Ridiculous," chimed Sinclair.

The deputy ignored that. His slitted eyes skipped about the room, missed Wentworth in concealment.

"Where's the fake government agent?" the deputy demanded.

"Fake!" It was a gasp from Sinclair, echoed angrily by Black. Unconsciously their eyes swung to Wentworth behind the door.

The deputy cursed. Even as he sprang forward into the room, gun pivoting toward Wentworth, a man's heavy feet pounded up outside the cabin.

"They found a murdered man in the mine. Got a Spider seal on him!" he shouted. "That fake government dick is the Spider!" **WENTWORTH'S SECRET** was out. This deputy and at least one assistant out there were ready to seize the Spider. Within the cabin also were two men who would probably side with the deputy and act against him. In their minds would be only the thought that the Spider was a criminal, that he might well be a spy of the Silver Syndicate which they blamed for all these deaths and disasters. Yet Wentworth must escape. He must carry on his work, foil these colossal plotters.

Escape would be simple enough if this leather-faced deputy with the gun were a criminal. Wentworth could easily beat him to the shot, put his lead through the man's heart. But the Spider did not battle police that way, any more than a soldier would shoot his own comrade-in-arms. The Spider and police were on the same side in their eternal war against crime, it was only that their methods were different—and the methods the Spider employed branded him a criminal in the eyes of the law.

The critical nature of the situation, the necessity of escape sped Wentworth to the attack. His hand was already planted against the open door. As the leather-faced deputy sprang forward, Wentworth thrust the door violently. It fanned at the deputy. He staggered to escape it throwing up his gun. He was not quick enough. The edge of the door struck his gun and battered it aside. The deafening blast from the revolver only buried lead in the wall.

Before the man could recover to point his gun again, Wentworth was upon him. A swift punch straight from the shoulder and the deputy spilled to the floor, out cold. A kick slammed the door in the face of the second officer. The bar fell into place automatically and Wentworth wedged it down tightly. He faced Sinclair and Black with a gun in his hand.

"I am the Spider," he said swiftly. "I am fighting the Syndicate and I am for you, Black. You must go with me. Get out that window."

Black had been taken by surprise by the swiftness of the action. It was apparent to Wentworth that the man was a consummate actor or actually had been dazed by the deputy's charge that he had murdered the paymaster.

Sinclair was the first to recover. He took short steps forward, remarkably light steps for a man of his bulk, steps that showed the strength of his massive body.

"You're staying here," he said thickly. "Black didn't kill that man. He has no reason to run away. It's a frame-up and you're a spy of the syndicate."

Wentworth could not wait to argue. The deputy was pounding furiously on the door.

"You can't escape," the officer bawled. "The cabin is surrounded. Open the door and surrender or it'll go hard with you." Sinclair's eyes flicked toward the door and Wentworth leaped. Sinclair sprang back, but he was not fast enough. The Spider's clubbed automatic smacked him to the floor.

"Hurry, Black!" Wentworth snapped, his voice low. "Get to the window."

Up to this time, neither the girl nor Black had moved, but now the girl clung to the miner.

"Don't go," she pleaded. "It's a trap. You didn't murder that man."

Wentworth cursed softly. He moved forward warily, automatic raised. "I don't like to hurt ladies," he warned, "but if I must...."

Black cursed and sprang at him. Wentworth ducked aside, tapped the man's temple lightly with the muzzle of the automatic. It was not enough to knock him out, but it sent him reeling weakly against the wall. The Spider seized Bessie Kendal, spun her about, her back to him, and lifted the gun menacingly, over her head. He didn't want to employ these methods but they were forced on him. Damn it. They had to get away! *Now!* Black's back was against the wall. He peered blearily at the two.

"Going with me, Black?" Wentworth demanded. "Or shall I tap Bessie on the head and make you?"

Black pushed off from the wall, stumbled. The rage of helplessness contorted his face.

"Do we go?" Wentworth persisted.

"No," Bessie said. "No, don't go, Harry! He won't hurt me!"

Wentworth's eyes met Black's. They stared fixedly. "She's right," Wentworth said flatly. "I wouldn't. But when I tell you you must go away, I'm telling you the truth."

Black continued to stare at him while the deputy pounded and shouted outside. Slowly he nodded. "I'll go," he said.

Wentworth reached the door in a stride. The deputy battered upon it with his gun. "Open up," he shouted, "or I'll smash it in. I'm covered by a half dozen guns."

THE SPIDER smiled bleakly. "Like hell you are," he muttered. "You talk too much about it." He eased the bar up, yanked the door open abruptly. A fat man with a face reddened by sun and exertion stumbled forward. Wentworth's gun swished and the man slumped to the floor.

"Outside, Black," Wentworth snapped. "There aren't any more deputies."

The miner reeled toward him. Wentworth seized his arm and they circled the cabin, found horses picketed in the shrubbery. Wentworth heard feet behind him, whirled. Bessie Kendall leveled the deputy's long-barreled revolver.

"You're not going to do it," she panted. "You're *not!* Harry doesn't know what he's doing."

"You little fool," Wentworth blazed. "Don't you realize that the syndicate has framed Black?"

The girl's blue eyes were sparkling with anger, her breath came fast between parted lips and her breasts jerked at the white tautness of her blouse. "You're not!" she insisted. She lifted her left hand in a pleading gesture. "Please," she said. "I know he didn't do it, and…."

Wentworth s eyes narrowed on a diamond solitaire that gleamed on the girl's left band. He pointed at it. "Some of the money that was stolen from the dead paymaster paid for that ring," he said bitterly. "Whether Harry killed him or not; that's the way the evidence stands. Think he can get out of it?"

The girl looked at the ring. Wentworth sprang and wrenched the gun from her hand. "What I said is the truth," he snapped. "Get back to the cabin and see if you can send those deputies in the wrong direction. Tell them the way we went and they'll think you're *lying.*" He whirled down a sharp embankment to where the horses were picketed.

"Go back, dear!" Black called, "the Spider knows best."

Wentworth vaulted to the saddle without fondling the stirrup, slapped the horse's neck with his hand and shot down a narrow twisting trail, Black at his heels. The Spider was an expert horseman, as indeed he excelled in all sports and athletics. He sat lightly in his saddle, swaying with the sharp carves, of the trail, ducking the slapping branches of low-hanging trees.

Once he glanced behind and saw that Black was riding hard on his heels. Then he gave his horse full rein. In five minutes at the most, those deputies would be on the trail. The Spider must be not only out of sight, but out of hearing by that tune.

At the base of the mountain into which the Silver Lode tunneled, he swung sharply to the right, winding up into the mountains. Five miles to the south and east was Leadville. Denver lay north. Behind them, misty with distance as they bored further and further into the hills, rose the high lonely crag of Pike's Peak.

Twice they saw men in miner's garb who stared at them curiously. Once, far in the distance, Wentworth heard signal shots, but after three quarters of an hour of a driving gallop, he called a halt beside a small stream to rest the horses. Black swung down immediately from his pony and faced the Spider, black eyes hostile and demanding. There was a scrawl of dried blood across his cheek from the blow on his temple.

Wentworth waited for no questions. He plunged directly into a full history of Black's case; told him about the tracing of the currency. One fact he withheld—that the murders in Washington and in Denver were committed in identically the same way.

"What have I gained running away?" Black demanded, speech clipped. "Looks like I'm guilty."

Wentworth's month thinned grimly. "If the police knew what I do about what happened at the mine today" he said shortly, "they'd hang you out of hand."

"What do you mean?" Black demanded. He took a tense half-stride forward, fists clenched.

Wentworth did not retreat nor did he make a move to draw his automatic. He turned his head aside an instant, listening for sounds of pursuit. A blast rumbled off to the south. The horse's blowing was noisy in the still close hotness of thee sun, but that was all. Had they shaken off pursuit? Wentworth turned to Black again.

"I mean," he said quietly, "that two attempts were made to murder me in the mine. A boulder was thrown at me as I climbed down the shaft ladder. On the level where you were working, a man attempted to kill me with a pick. That was the man they found at the bottom of the shaft with my seal on his forehead."

Black stared at Wentworth incredulously. "But why," he demanded, "should anyone attempt to kill you?"

"That," said Wentworth, meeting his gaze narrowly, "is what I'm asking you."

"Why, damn you—" Black's eyes' snapped with anger, but the calm regard of the Spider stopped his words, quieted him. "Believe me," he said, "I know no more about those attacks than you."

WENTWORTH STUDIED the man's lean-jawed face, probed his eyes with his own. Once more he felt that the man was sincere—or was an excellent actor. He could not be sure which. He did not see, however, how this man could profit personally from all the machinations in Washington and the silver states. Nor did he see how he could obtain the money to finance such a wide-flung conspiracy.

"This is my theory," Wentworth said. "If it's true that you did not kill the paymaster—and I am inclined to believe you did not—then some one is attempting to discredit you. You did purchase that ring from the jeweler?"

Black nodded, frowning. "I saved a long time for that," he said. "After I met my payroll, it looked like I'd have my head above water for a while and I took what I had left and got the ring."

"The case against you is damaging," Wentworth pointed out "You have been in hard lines for quite a while. Suddenly you buy a diamond ring and the money is the same that was stolen from a murdered paymaster. Wait—" he held up a hand as Black started heatedly to interrupt. "It's obvious that someone substituted the stolen money for yours." The Spider thought a moment.

"Then, today, I went to the police station in Denver and got them to hold off on your case until I talked to you. Someone in headquarters apparently warned certain men at your mine by phone. They attempted to kill me. If they had succeeded they would undoubtedly have put the blame on you. Thus they would have had you not only for the paymaster murder but also, supposedly, for the murder of a government agent. You see how the plot was woven?"

"But good God!" Black's voice was a hoarse whisper. "Why? Why?"

Wentworth shrugged. "Perhaps to steal your mine, to force you to sell. But it seems rather elaborate for so simple a thing. There's more to it than that, I feel sure."

He listened once more for signs of pursuit and thought he caught a faint shout off to the northeast. He turned to the horses, began tightening his saddle-cinch. "We've got to get going," he said abruptly. "They've probably got a posse on our heels by now."

Black nodded and they cantered through a wood of scattered hemlock where the thick needles would leave small trace of their passage. As they rode, Wentworth swiftly sketched a plan of action. Black was to remain in Denver and the vicinity—Wentworth would contrive simple disguises—and investigate any further mine disasters.

"Don't worry about your mine," Wentworth said. "I'll see that you get proper financing after this trouble is settled."

They pushed on through the hills. Twice they dodged search parties and finally, after dark, they abandoned the horses and made their way to the outskirts of Denver. There, when Wentworth had disguised Black and altered his own appearance, they separated.

Wentworth registered under an assumed name in a hotel and, once in his room, set speedily to work. He had a sense of impending disaster, an intuitive feeling that he tried to argue away. They had slipped successfully through the guard thrown about the city. In the morning, he would be gone, flying to Chicago. Nevertheless, the uneasy feeling persisted.

He walked to the window and peered out at the star-spangled sky, glanced down at the auto-thronged street. He shrugged impatiently at his thoughts, turned to the telephone. He had promised to call Bessie Kendall for Black and he had several other messages to deliver. From her, he learned that the man who worked at the head of the shaft, the one who undoubtedly had tried to kill him with a boulder, was dead. He had slipped and plunged down the shaft to his death. Wentworth's eyes grew hard at that information. Failure, it appeared, was promptly rewarded by the Assassins—also, they had wiped out a lead Wentworth had hoped to develop. He had intended to slip out to the mine again, but now that would be a useless risk.

His lips were grim as he made a reservation on the morning plane to Chicago, called his Hindu body servant, Ram Singh, In Washington, and, in staccato Hindustani, told him to find whether Roscoe Sinclair had any connection with the silver lobby. Then he lay back across the hotel bed and put in a call for New York. For the moment his mind was clear, but abruptly his hunch of impending trouble prodded him again.

He shifted impatiently on the bed. Of course trouble threatened. Didn't it always haunt the footsteps of the Spider? But it was more than that, a sense of—*pursuit*. Swiftly he checked over his movements since leaving the mine. It would have been possible, of course, for trackers to ferret out his trail, but the two men who had entered the city were vanished now with the help of disguise. Black did not know where he was or what he looked like… Impatiently, Wentworth thrust the thought from his mind.

RELAXED ACROSS the bed, right ankle across left knee, smiling at the ceiling... he did not see the ceiling. He saw the dear face of a girl hundreds of miles away in New York, of Nita van Sloan, the one woman in the world who knew the secret of the Spider.

It was nearly midnight. He knew how he would find her, lounging upon the seat of her wide studio window which, high above Riverside Drive, looked out upon the light-shimmering bosom of the mighty Hudson. He closed his eyes. She would be dressed, probably, in those pajamas of golden imperial silk which he had brought her from China. Dim lights would glint upon the bronze chestnut of her curls, her eyes....

"M'aime," he murmured softly into the phone as her glorious sweet voice came over the wires. The grim lines about his mouth softened, the always wary glint of his eyes became tender.

"Where are you, Dick?" Nita asked swiftly. "Senator Reagh phoned me just an hour ago that Calthoun had been murdered, strangled the way Racktat was."

Wentworth's hand tightened about the telephone. His eyes flew wide.

"They're keeping it secret as long as possible," Nita's voice hurried on. "They hope to catch the murderer and put an end to the terrorism."

There was no tenderness in Wentworth's face now. Thus it was always. These two, Nita and Wentworth, were capable of great love as only great spirits can be. There was between them an unwavering loyalty and devotion, but rarely, very rarely did they have even a stolen moment they could call their own.

Marriage was denied them. Wentworth had set his face sternly against it. What man with death and disgrace hanging hourly over his head would involve a wife in his shame? What man in those circumstances would dare to have a home, to have children? Such intuitive dread as haunted him tonight, that feeling of pursuit, would darken their happiest hours. No, such felicities were not for them. Wentworth had chosen the stern path of duty, of service to humanity. He did not, could not, regret that choice, but the cruelty of his and Nita's separation twanged harshly at his heart strings sometimes.... Even this moment of conversation could not be theirs. The hand of conspiracy and murder had thrust between them. His feeling of impending danger came back.

"It is wise to keep it secret," he said briefly, "but I'm afraid they won't succeed in finding the murderer that quickly. The conspiracy extends even to Denver." He told her briefly of the mine disaster. *"Attende, cherie.* Listen, dear." He lapsed into swift French. "Will you go to Chicago and get entrance to the home of Roscoe Sinclair. He has a girl ward, I believe, and it should not be too difficult. No, I don't know just yet what information I want there, but many suspicious things point to him. Yes...."

He broke off, listening to her rapid words telling him more details of the Washington situation. His head jerked abruptly on the pillow, his eyes flashed to the door. He caught a rasping of metal. His gaze narrowed as it fixed on the doorknob. It was turning slowly! The danger he had sensed, the pursuit he had felt near, had overtaken him!

Abruptly he realized what must have happened. That call

to Bessie Kendal… Police must have tapped her phone. Good Lord! In that conversation he had identified himself as the Spider!

CHAPTER 3
SINCLAIR SMILES

WENTWORTH EASED off the bed, getting quietly to his feet, his eyes warily on the door. It was locked, of course, but a smashing assault would break it in.

"All right, darling," he said softly into the phone. "I'll see you soon."

He severed the connection, replaced the telephone carefully on its cradle.

"Of course I love you, darling," he said aloud, pretending to continue the telephone conversation. The knob had ceased turning now and he saw that the door was straining in its frame. Someone was thrusting heavily, silently, against it from the outside, hoping to force it in and take him by surprise.

"I always miss you, dearest," Wentworth said. "You know that." There was a mocking smile upon his lips. Swiftly he gathered up his coat, thrust a hat into his belt—he wanted them to see the red wig he wore—still talking as if into a telephone.

The door was swelling at the bottom. Evidently a powerful jack had been applied to it there. Within minutes it would burst inward.

Wentworth mounted a small table that stood close to the door jamb. He squeezed his body against the wall, reversed his automatic in his hand. Yes, it was clear enough now, the tracing of that phone call. He had considered that possibility but had doubted that the county authorities would act so quickly. Probably the federal agent had advised them. These would be police outside the door, men against whom he could not use his weapons.

But he must escape. This far-flung conspiracy had already struck again in Washington. There was no end to its daring criminal operations. The grip as it was establishing on Congress could not be lightly broken. It might be turned to any foul purpose. The extent of the plotters' progress was clear in the action of Senator Reagh—concealing a murder to prevent the spread of terrorism!

Wentworth's jaw clamped rigidly. These police must not be allowed to stop him! The door at his elbow groaned with pressure; abruptly a heavy blow crashed against it. The lock snapped in the hands of the officers and as they reeled forward wildly, twisted their heads toward the phone. Wentworth was on the opposite side of the room. The instant the door crashed inward, he seized the lintel above the door and swung his body out into the hall, gun in his teeth. Two other men in the hall were taken totally by surprise. Before their gaping mouths could fashion a sound, before they could more than start their hands toward their guns, Wentworth was upon them. His gun flicked twice and he was racing down the hall at top speed, leaving two policemen unconscious on the floor.

Voices bellowed out behind him as the two who had crashed

through the door discovered the trick. "Quick!" one shouted. "Phone the dick in the lobby!"

Wentworth smiled slightly. He raced up two floors, taking steps lightly two and three at a time. During that swift climb, he snatched the red wig from his head, slipped hard rubber discs which had distended his cheeks out of his mouth and into his pockets. A brisk rub with a prepared cloth he always carried and the ruddy complexion he had assumed gave place to his normal healthy tan. He set a hat jauntily upon crisp black curls.

For the first time since he had reached Denver, he was in his real character, Richard Wentworth, the wealthy clubman and sports enthusiast, sometime dilettante of the arts, amateur criminologist, of New York, of Nice....

He walked calmly to the elevators and pressed the signal button. There was a virile self-reliance about the man who waited there in the hall for the cage—a sturdy set to his well-built shoulders, a confident arrogance to the poise of the head. There was, too, an appearance of wealth and well-being. He sauntered into the elevator, strolled out on the ground floor past the furious watchful eyes of the police. Wentworth glanced curiously at the beefy detective who had crashed through the door into his room a few moments before, smiled slightly at his perspiring face, walked out of the hotel, and caught a taxi to the railway station.

He could charter no special plane here; the fields would be watched. But how could police, looking variously for a thin-faced man with a beak nose and a redhead with wide, plump face, spot the Spider in this quiet, confident Richard Wentworth? They couldn't! He took a compartment to St. Louis, caught a plane to Chicago and landed in that city the following afternoon.

THE AFTERNOON papers screamed with two sensations: the murder of Senator Calthoun and the charge that the Spider had blown up a silver mine, rescued a murderer from three posses—Wentworth smiled. Were there that many chasing them?—and slipped through the fingers of the Denver police when they crashed into his hotel room. The city was literally surrounded by police, the story went on. This time the Spider would not escape.

He smiled at that, too, briefly. He had not yet been able to escape that sense of impending disaster. It shadowed him like a faithful but sinister dog. He glanced back over his shoulder as he stepped into a taxi. That hatchet-faced man with the odd taste in ties. Hadn't he seen him in the hotel lobby today?

Wentworth cursed impatiently. The Spider had never been afflicted with nerves before! He sought to shrug off the depression that harassed him, but it clung clammily as he buried himself in the paper once more. Two stories on the inside pages seized his attention.

In Nevada the previous day, two mines wrecked by disasters had been bought by the Sinclair Syndicate which was, said the paper, providing work humanely, for the miners making repairs; in Washington, free silver advocates were demanding that the money of the nation be based equally on silver and gold. President Roosevelt had denounced the proposal as ruinously inflationary, but the political dopester who wrote the story said there was every, reason to believe the bill would go through.

Wentworth crushed the paper in his fist, glanced out the window of his taxi at the brawling traffic. They left the Loop, whipped north. There was a red-and-black taxi not a block behind them. It was still there as they careened along Michigan Boulevard. Wentworth cursed softly. Perhaps it was his nerves, but he would swear he was being followed. He jerked his head angrily. There could be no tie-up between Richard Wentworth and the Spider's activities in Denver. He was imaging things. Yet the Spider was not given to hallucinations. Grimly, he set himself to watch the other cab.

Wentworth was headed for the Gold Coast, for the home of Roscoe Sinclair. A telegram from Ram Singh had awaited him in Chicago. It stated that Sinclair made little pretense of concealing his financial support of the silver lobby.

Wentworth's eyes narrowed as he realized the cunning of such a stand. If the head of the silver syndicate actually were behind these atrocities and Sinclair were to insist righteously that he had no hand in any of the propaganda—and if despite that pose, the lobby were traced to him, all the evil might be laid at his door. But if he openly financed the lobby, people would believe his operations went no farther.

Wentworth was calling on Sinclair in his true identity. He had been openly cooperating with certain Washington officials in an effort to combat the conspiracy and thus had a legitimate entrée to the Sinclair home. The cab swung into the private driveway that traced a geometrical semi-circle into the walled garden of Sinclair's huge masonry pile. Wentworth paid off the driver, climbed the broad steps deliberately, cane and gloves in hand.

He paused at their head, glancing at the Boulevard. The red-and-black cab whirled around the corner out of sight, but Wentworth could have sworn he glimpsed the hatchet-faced man in it. His lips pressed firmly together. Was it possible that he had slipped up somewhere in his flight? That police had followed from Denver? But if that were so, why did they follow instead of acting? He wondered as he punched the doorbell.

There was some difficulty, of course. Strangers rarely called on the Silver King without appointment, but in the end he was admitted to the vast room that Sinclair called a study. It had a huge Gothic fireplace; the walls were studded with trophies of an African hunting, trip; there were bookcases—and behind a hand-carved desk of teak that spread its mass across a bay window looking upon Lake Michigan sat the Silver King himself.

The chair he occupied was massive, too, like the room, but it seemed a suitable throne for the man. His Communist son was, if anything, smaller than the father, his shoulders less massive, his chest not quite so deep, his broad-boned face and head smaller. The Silver King had the same recalcitrant harsh hair as his son, but the father's was pure white—it was not for his rich mines alone that he was known as the Silver King.

The man rose behind his desk and seemed to dwarf its solid strength. "I have heard of you, Mr. Wentworth," he said, and his voice was deep as a bell, resonant. "They told me along the

Congo that B'wana Wentworth had stopped the charge of the biggest bull elephant ever seen there with one shot." He—gestured toward the far end of the huge room where the shoulders and mounted head of an elephant protruded from the wall as if the animal had burst through. "I had to be content with a small cow."

THE MAN'S manner was gracious, yet it seemed to Wentworth that there were overtones in his voice as if the man secretly mocked him. His premonitions again? Well, his hunch had been fulfilled in Denver! He stepped close and clasped the wide-palmed hand the Silver King offered, searched the intelligent, forceful countenance. There was driving power there and ruthless will. In the eyes, too, Wentworth thought he sensed mockery. Inwardly he was tensely alert, his mind was wary, but when he spoke, it was carelessly, referring to his killing of the elephant.

"It was a lucky shot," he said. "I am trying for another lucky shot today."

The smile of greeting was gone from Wentworth's face now, and it was set, determined. There was driving power and ruthless will too. If Wentworth's face was more humane, if his eyes could hint at kindliness, it did not weaken his countenance. The towering bulk of the other man, his forceful personality, could not dwarf Wentworth.

Sinclair regarded him fixedly, the smile still lifting his mouth corners though his eyes were bleakly alert. "You speak in cryptograms, Wentworth," he said courteously, and once more Wentworth was aware of mockery. They were both as alert as duelists behind their rapier points.

"I'll decode," Wentworth said, words clipped short. "You are financing the silver lobby in Washington. Whether you are behind the atrocities that accompany its work I do not know, but you profit by them!"

Sinclair frowned. "I'm afraid I don't understand," he said quietly. Mockery was gone from his voice now, but there was an ominous ring in its place.

"Two senators have been murdered," Wentworth said curtly. "They were both opposed to silver legislation. Congressman Winkle's daughter was kidnapped and afterward he changed his stand on silver. Senator Fulcrim received a ten-thousand dollar equity in a silver mine—and changed."

Sinclair's eyes were widening slowly, the whites glinting around black irises.

Wentworth pounded on with the chronicle of crime and atrocity, cited the destruction of mines in Nevada which the syndicate had purchased. "Whether you are responsible for these things personally," Wentworth concluded harshly, "I do not know. But you and the syndicate are reaping the benefits. I call on you to denounce these practices and to throw your influence against them."

While Wentworth talked, Sinclair had seemed gradually to increase in height. The stiffening of his back added a full inch. His chest swelled and dark blood congested his face. His right hand had been resting on the back of the chair and the joints creaked with the force of his clenching fingers.

Wentworth looked him up and down slowly, lifted his eyebrows slightly. There was always a hint of mockery in those brows. When he arched them, when his eyes became slightly amused, it was downright insulting.

His wordless raillery touched off the gathering storm of Sinclair's anger. He roared out an inarticulate oath, stuttered. He pounded on the desk and finally managed coherent words. "You dare to infer I might participate…" His voice became hoarse. He swallowed, twisted his head. He flung out a rigidly pointing hand toward the door. "Get out!" he thundered.

Wentworth shook his head slowly. "You and I have things to talk over first," he said quietly. "You have not yet answered my request. If you—?"

Sinclair roared at him again and Wentworth raised his voice clearly above the thundering of the Silver King.

"If you refuse to pronounce against such measures," he declared, "I shall publish the facts in every paper in the country!"

Sinclair took two quick strides forward, light and muscular, and loomed over Wentworth like a colossus. It was not that he was taller than Wentworth. Actually they were the same height. But the man's girth was so immense, his shoulders so broad, that he seemed literally a giant. His fists were clenched at his sides. He raised them, trembling above his head.

Wentworth did not retreat an inch before the menace of the man. He stared, calm-eyed, into the angry face, then he slipped a cigarette from his case and lighted it with the snap of the platinum lighter whose base held the dread calling card of the Spider.

If you're not careful, Mr. Sinclair," Wentworth said quietly, mouthing smoke, "you're going to have an attack of apoplexy.

I'm quite sure your physician has warned you against getting excited."

For seconds the Silver King still threatened Wentworth with his clenched fists, then abruptly his passion evaporated. It seemed to leave him tired. He moved ponderously to his desk and punched a white button viciously.

"I'll request that you go now, Mr. Wentworth," he said coldly. "I regret that I lost my temper, but you'll admit the provocation was extreme."

Wentworth shrugged, funneling smoke from his nostrils. "You still have not given me my answer," he reminded.

Sinclair put both hands on his desk and leaned forward, heavy shoulders ominous.

"The answer," said Sinclair, "is *no*. As to your threat to publish my refusal in the newspapers, I do not think that it would be advisable, Mr. Wentworth." He leaned even more, so that his elbows flexed, so that he almost touched for an attack. He whispered his final words. "Or shall I call you by another and a shorter name, Mr. Spider!"

SINCLAIR HISSED the word Spider and for moments after he spoke, the room seemed full of the sound. It thudded into Wentworth's heart with the impact of a rifle bullet, but he merely raised his brows at Sinclair, blew smoke toward the high-beamed ceiling. His mind was racing. In heaven's name, what did Sinclair know? The information of his identity could net haste fallen into his hands. If Sinclair were at the head of these atrocities, if he directed this ruthless Silver Band, that knowledge was a fearful weapon.

Dispassionately, Wentworth considered whether he was justified in taking this man's life. He certainly would not kill to protect himself alone. But if this man actually directed the operations of the Assassins, his life was forfeit a hundred times over. And preservation of the Spider was more than a personal need to survive. The Spider alone had been able to save the nation from peril in countless encounters with the Underworld. It appeared now that even his masterly strategy was at a loss. How then could the ordinary officials of justice hope to succeed? Coolly, Wentworth studied Sinclair. Was he guilty?

"I assume," said Wentworth, "that you mean to charge me with being the criminal who calls himself the Spider?"

Sinclair-smiled with tight lips. "I'll do more than charge," he said, "I'll prove it."

"Interesting," Wentworth murmured, snapping his cigarette into the Gothic fireplace. "I've always admired the chap. I have been confused with him before, but this is the first time proof has ever been offered. But we are straying from the point. Your decision not to oppose these criminals is final?"

Sinclair nodded, black eyes intent on Wentworth. "Why should I kill the goose that lays the silver egg?" he asked blithely. "I have nothing to do with their operations and they bring me big profits."

Wentworth sighed. "Too bad I'll have to publish." He turned on his heel, sauntered toward the door. "Will you have your man bring me my hat and stick?"

"Just a minute, Wentworth." Sinclair's heavy voice was

portentous. "You understood fully what I said? *I have proof that you are the Spider!*"

Wentworth turned at the door.

"I quite understand," he smiled. "The police will pay you fifty thousand dollars for it, if it will convince a jury—rewards, you know."

Sinclair took quick steps across the room. "The evidence involves your paramour," he said, sneering. "Nita van Sloan."

The flat of Wentworth's palm caught Sinclair's cheek with a crack like a pistol shot. Powerful though the Silver King was, he reeled under the blow. He steadied himself, black eyes blazing from a face that was dead-white except for the spreading red where Wentworth had struck.

"Now I shall not wait to give that information to police," he said. His breath came heavily through his nose.

"You may do as you wish about that." Wentworth's voice was cold and level. "But if you besmirch the name of the woman I love, I shall make a point of killing you if I have to smash through seventeen line of police to do it." A thin smile lifted his mouth corners. "If you believe that I am the Spider, you know that I am able to do precisely that."

Under his steady regard, Sinclair's glaring eyes widened. He fell back a pace and his hand flew to his coat pocket—a gun undoubtedly. Yet Wentworth had not moved, had only looked at him with his piercing gray-blue eyes. Still holding his gaze, Wentworth bowed stiffly from the waist.

"Au 'voir," he said lightly. "I'll be seeing you—again."

He strode from the baronial hall and the study door closed

with a sullen thump. The butler stood rigidly with hat and stick in his hands. Behind the man, sliding doors were opened a slit. Wentworth swiftly interposed the man's body. Through such a slit, guns might speak!

CHAPTER 4
THE SPIDER IS CAUGHT

THE DOORS slid apart. A girl stepped out. The light behind her outlined a charming figure in a rose tea gown. Her hair, cut in a long bob, swung darkly graceful beside the slim column of her throat.

"May I see you a moment, Mr. Wentworth?" she asked "I am Elsa Willing, Mr. Sinclair's ward."

Wentworth bowed silently, eyes interested, and walked into the room. She rolled the doors together, leaned against them. Her face tapered to a pointed chin. Her eyes were black and so large it was difficult to look from them to the dot of a nose, the scrap of crimson that was her mouth. "I couldn't help hearing," she said swiftly. "Nita van Sloan was on the phone a little while ago and I am going to meet her for tea." She ran a hand over the heavy rose silk of her tea gown, smoothed its hang about her suavely modeled hips. "You have seen Tony and Harry?"

"Tony? Harry?" Wentworth's tones were gently inquiring. If this was a trap set by Sinclair to obtain a confession that he knew these two men, whom the Spider, not Wentworth, had met, he was going to be disappointed.

"Tony Sinclair, my father's adopted son," the girl explained rapidly. "And Harry Black, his friend."

Wentworth shook his head, smiling, "I'm sorry."

The girl's disappointment made her entire figure droop. "I'm—I'm very fond of them both," she said faintly. "And father won't permit a word about either of them." She straightened. "I'm sorry I detained you."

"A pleasure," Wentworth insisted, bowing. He left as soon as the butler had summoned a taxi and once more the red and black cab followed. The smile that played about Wentworth's mouth was far from pleasant. He was going to put an end to this trailing right now. With Sinclair's threat to publish "proof" that he was the Spider hanging over his head, he must assume a disguise immediately. But first, he must learn who was responsible for this pursuit.

As he passed the Blackstone hotel, Wentworth tapped on the glass, the cab swerved from the Boulevard to the curb. He strolled into the hotel and watching from a window, saw the hatchet-faced shadow who had such an odd taste in neckties, alight and saunter in too. Wentworth slipped his automatic from the holster to his right coat-pocket and as the shadow crossed to a deep davenport, Wentworth dropped onto the seat beside him, jammed the gun against has ribs.

The man turned a startled puffed face.

"I've been wondering," said Wentworth, "where you pick up those quaint neckties. We're going to take a little ride and you can explain in detail."

The man's mouth closed thinly. "Nothing doing," he said in

a raspy voice. "And don't think you can bluff me. You wouldn't stand a chance if you shot me in here."

Wentworth rose, bent over the man. His gun came out of his pocket and he jolted the butt to the jaw in a punch that didn't travel two inches. The man collapsed. Wentworth strode rapidly to the desk.

"My friend has fainted," he said excitedly, "He's subject to heart attacks and—"

The clerk's hand was already jabbing at a button. "I'll have a doctor in a moment, sir," he said. "Shall we take him to your room?"

Wentworth frowned, dug out a wallet. "I haven't a room here," he said, "but here's money for one. The name is Caspar Haggard."

He raced back to the unconscious detective. As he strode toward him, his hand slipped to a small kit he carried always strapped beneath his arm, He bent over the detective again and slid the needle of a hypodermic into his thigh.

When the doctor had carried the detective to a room, he made a puzzled examination. "No evidence of heart attack. He's not in danger, but…" he diagnosed, "the man seems to be under the influence of narcotics."

Richard Wentworth

Wentworth raised his brows. "So that's it! I didn't know Jim had... Not an overdose, is it, doctor?"

"Not enough to be dangerous."

Wentworth nodded. "I'll give him a talking to when he comes out of it. Thanks a lot, doctor." He went out with the physician. Half an hour later he returned and went over the detective's pockets. The man was a representative of the Carson Howe agency. His name was Hart.

Wentworth glanced at his watch. It would be four hours before he could gain unobserved access to the agency offices. But there was still work to do. Rapidly he returned to his own hotel and resumed the disguise of the red-headed man who had escaped Denver police, restored the florid complexion and pouchy cheeks, donned a flamboyantly cut check suit.

He registered at another hotel under an assumed name and began calling newspapers.

"This is the People's Anti-Silver party," he told each in a high, nasal voice. "We interviewed Roscoe Sinclair and asked him to pronounce against the criminal practices of the silver lobby in Washington."

He then quoted Sinclair's reply. "We realize," he went on, "that you can't print this on our say-so, but suggest that you interview him on the same subject."

WENTWORTH GLANCED at his watch again and found he had just time for a leisurely meal before he burglarized the agency offices. He found Nita had not returned to her hotel so he went out to eat.

He was no longer followed, he was sure, but Sinclair's threat kept him on the alert. That and his ever-present feeling of imminent danger. Never before in his adventurous career had he been thus harassed. It tautened his nerves, pulled his eyes sharply to every shadow he passed.

An hour and a half later, when he picked the lock of the Howe Detective Agency offices, his heart was pounding—and he gripped a blackjack in his hand. He scouted the entire suite, found it empty, and crossed to the safe. With the aid of a stethoscopic suction disc which he attached to its face, he opened the vault speedily and within minutes was skimming through the secret files!

Hart's assignment revealed the agency had been hired by Roscoe Sinclair! That discovery made Wentworth swear softly. If Sinclair were not one of the conspirators, at least he was extraordinarily interested in their activities!

Hart's card revealed that the agent had been assigned to trail "Richard Wentworth from arrival 2:15 p.m. at airport." A detailed description followed. Following up the ease number on that card, Wentworth read a carbon of a telegraphic report from Denver that related the occurrences at the Silver Lode mine of Harry Black, of the escape from the hotel of the red-headed man described as the Spider. Appended was a list of telephone calls he had made from the building and they included his conversations with Rani Singh and Nita van Sloan!

Wentworth cursed under his breath. So that was the evidence Sinclair held of his connection, with the Spider. Wentworth skimmed through other records of the case, found a detailed history of every mine accident, of every Washington atrocity. His eyes were like hard round agates, his lips bitter. He and Sinclair would have a showdown this night!

For a while he had believed the man innocent—a ruthless money-grabber—but innocent of the crimes. Now the situation was altered. He slid the file back into the safe, straightened to leave—and a voice rasped an order at him. "Lift the mitts, boy friend."

Wentworth's face tightened. He stiffened where he stood and slowly his hands went up. He dared not make a sudden move, for it would invite a bullet in the back. Damn it, he had played an amateur trick, had become so engrossed in his study of the files that he had allowed someone to slip up behind him.

Someone, but whom? That raspy voice sounded familiar. Wentworth thought swiftly. His disguise was good, the same he had worn in Denver at the hotel, and be had a black silk mask ever his eyes, but there was always the danger that his true identity might be discovered. Even if his disguise fooled police, the arrest for burglary would be unbeatable and the Spider must not be hampered now.

He had just obtained a valuable clue to Sinclair, one that demanded an immediate show-down. Yet he was trapped. He could not shoot for he did not fight with police or innocent parties. He might put them out of the way temporarily....

A hand touched his pockets, removed an automatic, whisked off the mask, and footsteps retreated quickly. "Okay, boy friend," the voice rasped. Turn around."

Wentworth turned slowly and looked into the narrowing eyes of the detective, Hart! There was brutal menace in that narrow-lipped mouth. Dark blood welled abruptly in the detective's face. He cursed low in his throat.

"Red hair, florid complexion, full cheeks," he said under his breath. "For Chrissake, you're the same guy that got away from the cops in Denver. You even got the same clothes. *You're the Spider!*"

Hart began to grin slowly, lips growing even thinner as they widened. "Well, this is a break!" He came forward on springy, alert feet. "Well, just see who you really are under that disguise, Mr. Spider."

Wentworth awaited his coming with bright, alert eyes, lips just curved in a smile. Hart saw that smile and checked his advance. He cursed. "I guess I won't, after all," he said slowly. "I'll just get police here and tell them about you."

He backed up to the desk, groping for a phone there. His gun was ready and he held it competently. Wentworth was too far from him for a charge. He was without a weapon that would span the distance between them and he knew well that if he was arrested, he could not explain away this burglary of an office safe. Once the police came, they would handcuff him, strip off the disguise—and Richard Wentworth would be revealed as the Spider. There was no definite proof on him, but the information in those secret files would make trouble, and if Roscoe Sinclair threw his weight into the case against him... Arrival of police would greatly reduce his chances of escape. Reduce! With a bark of scornful laughter, Wentworth mocked himself. They couldn't be reduced, because even now there was no chance at all!

Yet, he must escape if he was to pursue the evidence he had gained, if the ruthless Silver Assassins were to be held in check,

Nita Van Sloan

if their menace of dictatorship though a subsidized and terror-ized Congress was to be overcome.

Hart found the phone with his left hand, his eyes, his gun never wavering from Wentworth. He would not hesitate to shoot. He picked up the phone with a mocking twist to his lips.

With quivering muscles, his brain struggling frantically and vainly to find an out, Wentworth heard the detective speak into the phone. "I want a policeman," he said, "and I want him fast!"

ABOVE THE building where Wentworth, helpless at the

point of a gun, waited for the police, waited for the search that would reveal his identity as the Spider and permit the Silver Assassins to rage unhampered over the land, a twin-motored Curtis Condor was winging eastward toward Washington. Within the noise-insulated cabin, six men sat at conference and a seventh stood with his back to the shut-off forward cockpit.

The seventh was a massive man with a mane of silvery hair and he was smiling suavely. The man nearest him on his right took a black fat cigar from his mouth and poked it toward him. "It's swell, Sinclair, to talk about killing this Spider," he said. "But that guy is poison, plain poison to anybody that tries to take him for a ride."

The white-haired man nodded amiably. "There's just one thing to do with venomous creatures," he said curtly. "Either remove their poison sacks—or crush them. Other men who have fought the Spider know that all attempts to draw his fangs have failed. Nita van Sloan, his girl, is in Chicago. In fact, at this moment she is in a theatre with my ward. But it is useless to take her as a hostage." The leader gestured impatiently. "That's enough about the Spider. He's a minor matter. Let's get on with the plans."

A minor matter! No man ever before dismissed the Spider in that way. It was almost as if this man knew that even now Went-

worth stood helpless before a gun while police sped through the streets to unmask him.

The massive silver-maned leader looked slowly over the group. The man on his right put the black cigar back in his mouth, lounged in his seat. His name was "Machine-Gun" Maxer and he headed a murderous mob. Though he was relaxed, there was an air of perpetual physical alertness about him. He was thin, wiry with a repressed secretive mouth that seemed to fold in upon itself.

He twisted in his seat and looked over the others sitting comfortably in the plane. He knew them all by reputation, but this was the first time any power had united them all on the same side of the fence. There was "Pete" Daggar, with his scar-twisted face. The "Pete" was not short for Peter. It signified that he knew all there was to know about "pete" work, which is safe-cracking. Another little line of his was infernal machines of all descriptions; he was a specialist in explosives.

The oily fat man with the bulbous rouge-red cheeks was an unscrupulous blackmail magazine publisher. He was an expert in rumors, in spreading propaganda of all kinds. Jess Dartase had used his invaluable services in snatching a corner in copper some five years before. Jess Dartase had been caught in the end. The oily fat man had wriggled out.

There was that lean man of long hair and fervent eyes, a dark, emaciated face. Forster Simms, one of the best radical agitators that ever stepped upon a soapbox for his own selfish ends. He specialized in labor trouble, all kinds. He could make a satisfied shop revolt against an honest employer, or he could sway dissatisfied men into a thieving agreement with a rapacious boss—it all depended on where the greater profit lay.

The other two were mobsmen like Maxer himself, trained in the same hard school of murder and cut-throat warfare. That silky bozo there in a tuxedo specialized in killing of a *de luxe* type. "Machine-Gun" Maxie had heard it whispered about in his own mob that the murder mob had removed Senator Calthoun. Maxie turned from his slow inspection of his companions and regarded the white-maned Silver King before him. He rolled greasy blue smoke from his hard lips and smiled. It looked like something really big.

There were the allies the assassins had chosen and they were formidable. None more powerful existed in the underworld. Wentworth, standing at gunpoint hundreds of feet below them, would have gone cold with rage and despair if he could have known such forces of evil had been united.

The leader clipped the end from a pale slim perfecto, lighted it deliberately. "Maxie," he said. "Suppose we hear from you first."

Maxie rolled the black cigar between his fingers, pushed out a thick cloud of smoke, "I ain't got much to say, Sinclair," he reported gruffly. "If you want the Spider bumped, it's okay by me. Just say when the party is to come off and I'll do the rest." THE WHITE head nodded gravely. "Tomorrow night," he said quietly, "a plane full of senators will fly from Washington to Denver. At my invitation, they are making the trip to investigate conditions in the Colorado mines. I will contrive to have Wentworth aboard." He frowned down at the glowing tip of the perfecto. Smoke rose in a thin haze from it. "I want you, Maxie, to see that the plane is wrecked, and that it burns—completely." He looked up swiftly, blade eyes intent on the killer. "Understand?"

Maxie took the cigar out of his mouth. There was a tight smile about his thin hard lips. "You pick 'em big, eh, Sinclair?" It was not dissent. It was admiration. Maxie nodded his head slowly. "Check. You'll give me the dope on when and where?"

The leader nodded also. "These men who are going west are all opposed to my silver plans," he said steadily. "I have tried gentle means—kidnapping and bribery—without results. Nothing remains but to kill them. And picking them off one by one is too slow." He bowed slightly toward the silky slender man in tuxedo. "With all due tribute to your extreme efficiency with Calthoun, Ferrara."

The silky one smiled with a flash of sparkling white teeth beneath a dainty black mustache. "I take it, Señor Sinclair, that you still have work for me, eh?" he purred.

"There is a slight chance that the measure might be vetoed," said the massive leader. "I do not think the *Vice-President*, if he had the power, would dare veto."

Ferrara's face straightened with a suddenness that would have been comical had not stark ferocity glittered from his eyes. His curse was searing.

"Ees that an order, Señor Sinclair?" he asked softly, "or just a—what you say—perhaps?"

A slow smile answered Ferrara and the other five men sat tensely in their chairs staring at Sinclair's face. They were used to big things, these men—to big crimes, to cold-blooded murder—

but this man spoke calmly of assassinating the President of the United States! It was evident the leader enjoyed their tension.

"It is, for the present," he said, "only perhaps."

Ferrara nodded slowly, eased back in his chair. "I shall be ready," he said.

The leader's massive white head turned, the still black eyes stabbed at "Pete" Daggar. "What have you to report?"

Daggar's smile was distorted by that twisting scar down the left side of his face. "Three mines were wrecked today," he said with jerky words.

The killer said that simply, innocently, a report of a task well done to the master who had ordered its accomplishment. The master did not ask the details. He was not interested in those facts, nor in the wails of bereaved women, the silent, hard-lipped suffering of a hundred others who stood grouped about the shafts of the wrecked mines.

OUT IN the Colorado hills, two score women stand around a rope staked about a hole in the ground. Hooded flares coat the earth with brilliant white light, thrust their glare downward into the shaft, make little pebbles stand out vividly with their supports of black shadow. The loose eccentric engine chugs and strains and a rope rolls about a drum, lapping over layers of rope. It is a deep shaft.

Soundless, their strained faces even whiter in that brilliant glare, the women crowd against the rope now, watching, watching. The rope creaks, the engine chatters, an open-sided cage swings clear of the shaft and a dozen weary men climb off, others spring to the cage and it drops like a plummet. The engine idles.

The men go down by gravity, depending on the brakes of that drum.

The women break their silence, cries that are shrill with the tension of waiting. "How much longer?"

Other women stand with their arms, crossed high up, holding shawls about their thin shoulders. The nights are frigid in the Great Basin country. The days may soar above a hundred degrees, the night drops to forty. These women say nothing. They stare with that question in their eyes. *How much longer?*

A weary rescue-worker crosses to the rope and stands awkwardly before one of the thin-faced waiting women.

"They're still tapping, Ma," he says. "In another six hours we ought to know."

Six hours while workers bore through piles of solid earth and rock to find men entombed by a man-set blast. Six hours while the close air of their living tomb grows fetid and strangles them. Fifteen men down there in that tomb, hopeful and helpless....

The brakes of the engine shriek suddenly into the night, with the shrillness of a trapped animal. A half-mile down in the earth, a dozen men stream from the still bouncing cage, walk with swift slouching strides down a drive slung with emergency electric-lights. They take the picks from the hands of a dozen other men working there. Those men will go to the surface and another crew will descend. Two crews. They batter at the tomb of frantic men from two levels.

The tomb! It is a black hollow not four feet square, a dozen feet long. In that room encased by walls of living rock, fifteen men crouch on the floor, motionless, waiting. Like the faint ticking of a clock of doom they hear the urgent battering of the picks. Within they dare not stir, dare not use the one tool they have. Each movement will more swiftly use up the thickening air, absorb more of their starvation supply of oxygen. Sweat drops from them.

For six hours already they have been cooped up like this. Of their injured men, struck down by the sudden blast, two have died. Their corpses are crowded against the bodies of living men. Three hours ago, young Jack Bierkin went mad with waiting. They knocked him down and tied him up. He moans now in a corner. Sometimes he raises a thin cracked voice in a bawdy song. Perhaps, if they ever reach the sunlight, Bierkin will recover. His father was the one who knocked him down.

Clink... Thump... Clink.

The picks pecking at the rock-slide that seals their tomb. Faint sounds like the ticking of the clock of doom....

AND IN a plane above Chicago, Daggar with his scar-twisted smile, is reporting "Three mines were wrecked today," to the master who ordered these things so that he might own more mines, so that more wealth may pour into his pockets.

"You did well," says the white-maned master.

Far away in the hills of Colorado and Nevada women stand in the night and moan, *"How much longer?"*

"You did well," the master says to Daggar again. "What about the grenades?"

"They will be ready Labor Day," Daggar concludes and lounges back in his chair.

The leader turns next to the publisher. "I know how your

propaganda work is progressing. You had a difficult task, but I think you have succeeded in emotionalizing silver. You have paved the way well for Simms."

Next the agitator's report. "Tomorrow," Simms got to his feet and gestured angularly, his voice taking on platform timber, "we shall begin the march on Washington. On Labor Day, we shall be there. My Silver Battalions shall subdue the capital! My Battalions shall rule the nation!"

The leader cut him short with a chop of his cigar. "Your battalions will take my orders," he said shortly, "or perhaps Ferrara will find other work to do."

Simms turned his hot, excitable eyes upon the chief's black eyes, looked from that granite face to the faintly smiling countenance of Ferrara, the silky one.

"I theenk you would look nice with a broken neck, eh?" Ferrara purred softly.

Simms seemed unable to answer. He gulped and his prominent larynx slid up and down in his throat. He sat down. "Under your orders, of course, Sinclair," he muttered hoarsely.

"Then our plans are complete," the silver-haired one said shortly. "Maxie, and you two," he gestured toward the mobsmen, "will sprinkle your men in among the Silver Battalions. Daggar will supply the grenades. If the need arises, we will be in a position to take over the capital entirely."

He paused, smiling suavely. "I am aware that you men are interested only in the performance of the tasks I have stated, but I want you to realize the marvelous potentialities of the situation so that you will recognize that through me you may attain great wealth—but without me," his face grew stern, "nothing! Absolutely nothing!"

The six men stared at him without comment, the faces of killers. Maxie's harsh, alert gaze, Ferrara's smiling death, the distorted countenance of scar-faced "Pete" Daggar, the toothy oiliness of the publisher, agitator Simms still swallowing excitedly, feeling on his scrawny neck the cord of death. The leader seemed satisfied with what he saw.

"Once we pass the equal metal base bill," he said. "That is, the bill that puts silver on a parity with gold as a basis for money, we can push the price of silver higher and higher. By that time, the syndicate will control almost every mine in the country and many in other parts of the world. It means millions, millions… so long as we keep the capital in the palm of our hands."

He stretched out his two hands before him, palms upward and closed the fingers slowly. The fingers were thick and powerful. The killers watched them tighten, watched his wrists swell with strength. The hands dropped to his sides.

"That is all, gentlemen," he said. "I think you well see that loyalty will pay you good dividends."

An hour later, the plane landed and some of the men sped back to Chicago. Others took a plane eastward. Presently, the huge two motored Condor rose into the air and the white-maned leader sped on alone to Washington to wreck his atrocities, to plot the deaths of those legislators who stuck to their guns, who resolutely opposed his ruinous measures, seeing to what abyss they led the country.

"Machine-Gun" Maxie was in Washington, too. He was

preparing to wreck a plane in which many senators would plunge to their death—and the Spider, far away in Chicago, in imminent peril of death, had no inkling of their plans!

CHAPTER 5
THE MILL OF THE GODS

I N THE detective agency in Chicago, Detective Hart stood with his ready gun. He had held many men prisoner at pistol point, and he knew the reputation, the trickiness of the Spider. He was taking no chances on his escape.

Wentworth, raging inwardly at himself for permitting the capture, frantically sought a means of escape. But even Wentworth did not know how important it was that he snatch himself from this man's hands, how important that he speed to Washington to protect the nation from the diabolical plotters of the plane.

"Listen, Hart," Wentworth said. "I've got plenty of dough. Let me buy my way out of this. We can stage an escape…."

Hart laughed nastily. "Listen, buddy. I've called the cops and I ain't getting myself in bad."

Wentworth took two small steps forward, his hands gesturing.

"I'll give you five thousand dollars cash," he said. "Cash, Hart."

"Cash?" queried Hart, narrow eyes showing surprise. "Where'd you get it, out of the safe?"

"Don't be like that," Wentworth scoffed. "Your lousy agency hasn't had five grand in a month." He kept moving forward. "You can chuck the mask and gun in the safe and use them against me if I cross you up."

Hart lifted the revolver an inch. "Take four steps backward," he ordered, the words clipping out between thin lips. "We'll work it this way. You turn your back and face the safe. Just tell me where that five thousand is and if it's all right, maybe we'll deal."

Wentworth turned his back, talking over his shoulder. "Okay, okay, but make it fast," he said swiftly, "those coppers won't take an hour to get here."

As if in confirmation of his words, the low growl of traffic was disrupted by distant sirens. "Hurry!" Wentworth barked. He heard Hart's footsteps coming toward him cautiously.

"The money's in the inside pocket of my coat, on the right," Wentworth said.

He felt the knob of the gun jab into his back, felt the man's left arm come over his shoulder, move cautiously toward his pocket. A thin smile lifted Wentworth's mouth corners, but he did not attempt an attack. That dick's finger would be heavy on the trigger. He rolled his eyes down and saw the hand touch the wallet there, saw it stop and the gun jolted harder into his back. The hand withdrew and the feet retreated cautiously. Wentworth twisted his head.

"Is it all right?" he asked anxiously. "How about it, Hart? You got the money, now. How about it? You can put the gun and mask in the safe to make sure."

Hart laughed nastily. "Sure, I got the money." He motioned Wentworth away from the safe, tossed the mask and gun in there. "Now we got all the evidence together and we'll just wait for the cops!"

Wentworth pivoted on his heel, face twisted with anger he found hard to simulate. He narrowed his eyes against the lurking laughter in them.

"So you'd cross me, you dirty louse," he said tightly. "Okay, I'll tell the cops you took a bribe."

He took small, hard steps forward, and Hart thrust his gun out menacingly. Wentworth backed up fast against the safe, fright in his face. The safe door swung shut. There was a flat dull menace in Hart's eyes behind the gun.

"You can't shoot me!" Wentworth cried.

"No?" queried Hart, a nasty smile on his hatchet face. "The cops would give me a vote of thanks for rubbing out the Spider. Anyway, what did you try to escape for? Tell me that." His hand was tensing on the gun.

"I didn't try to escape," Wentworth protested as if horribly frightened. Capture was only a few short minutes away. The police cars were whining into the street now, sirens dying as they braked to a halt.

"Sure, you did," said Hart. His eyes opened wide and their menace increased, the conscienceless eyes of a killer.

"No, Hart," Wentworth told him swiftly, "it wouldn't get by. You can't shoot me and say I tried to escape. If I were escaping, you'd shoot me in the back. And you're not going to get me to turn my back again."

HART CURSED and came around the desk fast, treading lightly on his toes. Wentworth braced his shoulders up against the safe and kept on looking scared. He rubbed his thigh against the safe door handle and threw the bolt, rubbed again and turned the combination knob. The safe was locked now.

"Quit it, Hart," he pleaded. "Look, I gave you five grand and now you're trying to cross me up. It ain't right, Hart."

The man came up to him with mincing steps, gun close in at his side and gripped hard, hatchet face with slitted eyes half closed in a killer's mask. Slowly, Wentworth began to smile, letting his actual mirth show through.

"You see, Hart," he said softly, "you took my gun and it's too late to fire it and make it seem self-defense…."

The door opened in the outer office.

"You can't get away with it," Wentworth raised his voice. "I'll tell the police what I know about you. You took five thousand dollars from the Spider to cover up that killing out in Denver and when…."

The door thrust open and two uniformed policemen thrust in. Hart wiped the anger off his face, but didn't take his eyes off Wentworth. "This is the louse I caught frisking the safe," he said shortly. "He's…."

Wentworth began to talk rapidly. "Okay, take us to the station house, officer. I came here to hire a detective to help me work on some evidence I had against the Spider. I wanted to collect that fifty grand reward offered for him. I wanted the detectives to help me locate a private operative named Hart because I overheard the Spider bribing a private detective of that name."

"It's a lie!" Hart shouted.

"It's the truth," Wentworth insisted. "I came here to hire a

69

detective and when I came here and told my story, this guy says he's Hart and I won't get any further with my story. He says he's going to call police and then shoot me and say I was trying to escape. But I wouldn't turn my back."

The two cops stared from one to the other of the two men, frowning. "What the hell is this?" demanded one of them, a husky young blond who hadn't shaved that day.

"The man's lying," Hart said hoarsely. *"He's* the Spider."

"Search him!" Wentworth insisted. "I saw the Spider hand over a wallet with five grand in it and it had the initials C.H. on it. See if he hasn't got it on him new. This happened only about an hour ago."

Hart came out of his crouch slowly and spat toward a cuspidor. "Aw, hell," he said, trying to grin. "Listen, cop, I come down to the office, see, and find this guy kneeling in front of the safe that he's opened. I take him and call headquarters, that's all there is to it. His disguise is the same the Spider wore in Denver. His gun and mask are in the safe…" He pointed with his hand toward the safe.

The blond cop looked that way. "The safe's shut," he growled.

Hart jerked his head that way. His mouth fell open. "You told me to put that gun and mask in the safe and then you backed into it and locked it!"

Wentworth laughed out loud. "And of course," he sneered, "a detective always does what the burglar tells him to."

The two cops were facing Hart now, shoulders hunched. "Listen, dick," said the blond youngster, "I don't like the sound of this at all."

"Now, listen…" Hart began backing up.

"He's got the wallet in his pocket," Wentworth cried excitedly, "That's why he doesn't want to be searched."

The two cops had their backs turned toward Wentworth now and were going toward Hart slowly.

"Look," said the blond cop. He was rolling his shoulders. They were wide and powerful. "Look, dick, if you ain't got the wallet, just say so and we'll let headquarters argue this out."

"Stand back," Hart said nastily. "I don't let every cop comes around paw me over just because he feels like it."

"He's got the wallet," Wentworth goaded. "It's a dirty frame he pulled on me. Only I kept my back to the wall so he couldn't shoot."

The cops weren't paying any attention to Wentworth now. They were closing in on Hart who was backed up against the desk, still holding the gun.

"Put that gun down, dick," the cop ordered. His voice sounded excited. "Put it down, or, by God, I'll see that the whole damned agency is pulled." He kept talking and walking closer. "You wouldn't shoot a cop, dick. It isn't worth it. They'd get you sooner or later. Even for five grand it isn't worth it. You can't kill us all."

He sprang suddenly. Hart cried out, raised his gun and hesitated. The young cop's hand closed on his wrist and twisted. Hart let out a thin scream and the gun fell.

"Frisk him, Joe," said the young cop, panting a little.

The other policeman went over the man, found the wallet, thumbed green backs. "Geez!" he gulped. "There *is* five grand here."

"Initials?" barked the young cop, snapping bracelets on the chastened Hart.

"Yeah," said Joe. "They're C.H."

"By God!" the cop swore. "That's just what you said, fellah," he called over his shoulder. He turned talking. "Lucky thing you remembered those initials…" His mouth sagged open. He cursed and the other cop turned, too. "What's the matter?"

"The guy is gone!" The blond cop yelled. "Hold that dick, Joe!"

HE DARTED through the outer office, pelted into the hall and down stairs. When he plunged into the street, gun in hand, Wentworth grinned unseen from his seat in a passing trolley car. The wig was off now and in his pocket. He lifted a newspaper in front of his face and pretended deep absorption in a columnist's attack on the owners of fire, trap tenements and the officials who permitted such buildings as would cost twenty-six lives in two months' time….

It took him a half hour to reach the Sinclair residence again and this time, disguise resumed, he scaled the wall, evading the constant patrol of guards, and slipped into the servants' quarters.

He made his way, silent as the black shadows of the rooms through which he crept, into the main part of the house, then froze motionless behind a looming suit of medieval armor as he heard the door of the main entrance open. Two women entered. The soft glow of the overhead lamp gleamed on their white shoulders as they allowed cloaks to slip from them. Wentworth smiled beneath the black mystery of his mask.

Those two women were Elsa Willing—the ward of the Silver King—and Nita van Sloan!

"Will we see your father tonight?" Nita asked casually and Wentworth felt the old thrill of delight at the sweet tones of her voice.

"No," Elsa said. "Father is flying to Washington."

Wentworth stiffened in his hiding place. If the Silver King was in Washington, some new mischief must be brewing there! He must hasten after him, seek to learn what his purposes were. He would have to force a show-down at once.

If only Wentworth could have known what portended in Washington, if he could have overheard that heartless plotting in the plane and learned what hostile forces would converge soon upon the capital! But he did not know. As yet he only suspected the white-maned Silver King. It seemed to him important to reach Washington, but also it was important to steal a moment with Nita, to learn what information she had gleaned… and there were other reasons.

He watched the two girls stroll into the drawing room, then stole back the way he had come to the street. A half hour later, when Nita entered the taxi she had kept waiting at the curb, she let out a choked small cry, then laughed softly and, sitting down, seized the hands of the man who smiled from a corner of the seat.

"Oh, Dick," she murmured. "One of these days, my heart is going to stop dead when, you frighten me like that!"

Wentworth laughed softly, drew her close. "And here, all the time," he said, "I was thinking my unworthy presence made your heart beat faster!"

"Conceited!" Nita murmured. Her lips contradicted the word. They were lifted to his.

But it was only a moment that they stole there in the dark taxi, a moment snatched from the midst of peril and death and horror. Then Nita was talking rapidly, telling what she knew; that Sinclair had gone to Washington by private plane, that Elsa was his sole heir since the disinheritance of Tony, that Elsa thought Tony had been treated unfairly, that Elsa talked incessantly of a young mining engineer near Denver named Harry Black….

"Harry Black!" Wentworth caught up the name. "Do you mean she's in love with him?"

Nita nodded gravely. "Phenomenal," she said drily, "but true."

Wentworth frowned into the darkness. That put an entirely new light on the situation. If the girl were in love with Black, then Black could profit tremendously by the operations of the Assassins. He need only remove Sinclair and marry the ward. It lent reason, too, to the repeated attempts against Black's mine.

Roscoe Sinclair knew of his ward's infatuation for Black and was determined to wipe him out. Black, on the other band, might be on the inside of all the criminal activities—that clue of the strangled paymaster implicated him strongly—and intend to cash in on all the criminality by marrying the ward. He would be above suspicion in the matter because he was only a struggling young mine owner. Wentworth exhaled a slow, deep breath.

"That is intensely valuable information, dear," he said. "So much so that I want you to leave here and go to Denver and investigate Harry Black, owner of the Silver Lode, now disguised as a truck driver and living at a hotel on lower Colfax Avenue. He happens to be engaged to one Bessie Kendall. I'd like to know whether that's bona fide on his part, or whether it's just camouflage to cover up this other affair."

He was frowning at the taxi driver's head.

"You'll meet Tony Sinclair out there, too. Take Elsa along with you if you can. You might learn a lot by just watching her. I've got to go to Washington to check up on Sinclair and set a task for Ram Singh."

Two blocks further on, with a final kiss, with a wrench that wrung his heart, Wentworth left Nita again and stood staring after the vanishing red tail-light of the cab. Whenever he left Nita, his heart was torn anew with the knowledge that he might never see here again, that the sharp dangers of his constant conflict with the underworld might bring his death.

Nita was staring backward as long as her straining eyes could make out the shadowy figure upon the curb that was her love. If she could have known what was being plotted even then in the plane that sped eastward, she could not have torn her arms from her Dick's neck, could not have borne the separation....

WHEN WENTWORTH'S plane circled out over the Potomac and swooped to a landing at Hoover Field, Roscoe Sinclair already had been in Washington four hours. Wentworth knew that, but he did not know the need for haste, did not dream that open attack upon the Senators, upon the government, upon the President himself, threatened. Instead of searching out the white-maned Silver King, the Spider sped directly from the field to the home of Senator Reagh and found the doughty little southerner deeply absorbed in financial reports. He lifted a lined face, eyes haggard behind rimless nose glasses.

"What have you learned?" he asked in his soft, quick voice.

Wentworth dropped into a chair and lipped a cigarette. "The Spider is working with us," he said.

Reagh's tired blue eyes brightened. "That's the best news I've heard since this damnable conspiracy got under way. If he wins this time, though, he'll be capable of miracles."

Wentworth lighted the cigarette, drew in smoke. "I am convinced that Sinclair must be behind the whole plot, but when I saw the man personally, I was not sure."

He detailed his reasons for suspecting Sinclair, while Senator Reagh listened with pursed lips. He had been in Washington a long time, he was approaching seventy and the silver battle had stripped him of all his reserve strength. He fought on with nerve alone. He nodded at intervals during Wentworth's recital, but at the end he shook his head slowly.

"It's convincing," he said, "but no police official would act on it and you couldn't get an indictment. By the time we gathered evidence—" he shrugged. His eyes brightened a little, he took off his rimless glasses and tapped the desk gently with them. "There are twelve of us in the Senate," he said, "who still hold the balance of power. So long as we stick together…" His voice trailed off.

"They are making new assaults. I called Harper for our usual morning talk today and he told me he felt that perhaps we were wrong in holding out against the silver bill, that the people appeared to favor it." He dropped his glasses to the blotter and folded his corded, age-blotched hands. "I know what that means. The conspirators have got to him some way. Bribery is out of the question there, but he has a son of whom he is inordinately fond."

Senator Reagh's weariness crept into his voice. "The twelve of us are taking a trip to Denver to investigate conditions there over the Labor Day weekend." He smiled wryly. "We are to be Roscoe Sinclair's guests. We leave this afternoon at two. His plane."

Wentworth leaned forward intently. "There is no chance that the bill could be brought up in your absence?"

Reagh shook his head slowly. "We adjourned last night until Tuesday."

Wentworth frowned, snapped the cigarette out an open window. Even in his ignorance of the fiendish plan afoot, he sensed that some trickery lay here. Of course, it might be that Sinclair was merely making a gesture of good-will.

"Sinclair going with you?" he snapped.

Reagh nodded and Wentworth dug out another cigarette. He couldn't see that anything very grave could be attempted with Sinclair a passenger on the plane. He wouldn't openly reveal himself.

A knock at the door and a negro servant brought in a newspaper whose black headlines screamed. Reagh snatched the newspaper, staring at it, then let it droop to the desk.

"Only eleven of us will go to Denver," he said dully.

Wentworth seized the paper, gripping it with white-knuckled hands.

Another senator had been wiped from the rolls of the opposition to silver, strangled in the night. The two men stared at each other and there was helpless rage in their eyes, something very like despair. For weeks now, the nation's capital had been shivering beneath the Terror. Here and there a prominent man dropped from sight, and always the ranks of the anti-silverites were weakened.

"It's damnable," Wentworth swore. "You and I know of a dozen cases of blackmailed votes, of bribery. These murders mount. I can't see the end of this. Even if Sinclair could be taken care of, this plot would still smash on now with its own impetus. It isn't alone that this present bill would work havoc."

"It would," said Reagh in his quiet soft voice. "I tell you that six months after we pass this bill, our currency will be so debased that our foreign trade will be absolutely ruinous. The exchange…" He broke off, shaking his head.

"**THAT'S NOT** the worst of it," Wentworth said vehemently. "Don't you realize that with a throttle-hold on Congress, these men will stop at nothing? They are interested only in their own advancement. They'll continue to propose and pass bills for private gain until the nation is ruined! Look at this propaganda!" He tossed the paper before Reagh and pointed to a story on the front page.

SILVER MONEY OUR ONLY HOPE

A grave statement by a learned economist followed. It undertook to prove with many twisted statistics that keeping more money in circulation was the country's only hope, that the only way of getting enough in circulation was free coinage of silver.

It proposed to base the United States currency three-quarters on silver.

"And this," said Wentworth, opening the paper to an inside page.

OVERTHROW GODS OF GOLD—STEARN

The headline quoted a noted preacher, Burton Stearn. He waxed hysterical about demon capitalists who had set up the gold basis of money for their own selfish interests.

"Our only hope to smash this dominion of shame," he wrote fanatically, "is to tear it up by the roots. Let us have silver alone as the basis of our currency!"

A preacher was to deliver an hour's sermon on Sunday afternoon over a nation-wide hook-up on the subject, "Freedom of Man, Free Silver."

"That preacher," said Wentworth bitterly, "has two hundred thousand invested in silver futures. But if you published that fact, it would do no good. He has one of the most moving voices I have ever heard. He emotionalizes silver."

There wasn't a word about an interview with Sinclair. Perhaps he had left Chicago too speedily. Other items in the paper told of the gathering of the Silver Battalion, a group of unemployed men who would march into Washington Labor Day and demand that free coinage of silver be voted so that they could get jobs as miners and in factories which made miner's tools. Their leader preached the gospel of silver as the solution of all problems. His name was Forster Simms.

How Sinclair, reading this day's paper, must have chortled at the success of his drive! How the ready acceptance of his invitation to fly west by those eleven Irreconcilables of the Senate must have pleased him! By night that plane was to fall in flames—and the last opposition to his dominion would fall with it. The Silver Assassins would be the virtual dictators of America!

For hours, while armed guards patrolled the halls of Senator Reagh's home, he and Wentworth struggled with the problem, but without hope. Wentworth was suspicious of the invitation from Sinclair—he had been told that he would be welcome to accompany the senators—but he could not believe that the Silver King would dare invite the men, to harm them. It would be blatant, too open. Investigation and punishment would be sure to follow.

Finally Wentworth left Reagh—the senators' aging clasp was as firm as a boy's—and went to his hotel. He decided to postpone the show-down with Sinclair a few hours, hoping to find some definite proof. The mere fact that a detective agency reported to him on all silver activities was circumstantial evidence, but not conclusive. He wondered why Sinclair had not fulfilled his threat to expose him as the Spider. He did not flatter himself that the man feared him—fear would never be part of the Silver King's makeup.

A telegram from Nita informed him that Elsa had agreed to accompany her to Denver and that they were leaving in the afternoon by plane. Ram Singh spread reports before Wentworth and waited, anxious dark eyes never leaving the face of the master he worshiped. The reports were routine investigations which Wentworth had entrusted to the Hindu.

There was an inquiry asking the Indian government whether any suspected devotees of Kali, the Thugs, had come to the United States recently. The method of killing by a silken garrote thrown from behind—then a wrench which broke the victim's neck—was the Thuggee method. Thousands had died that way in India at the hands of these murderous highwaymen. The British government of India conveyed its compliments to Richard Wentworth, Esq., remembering his past favors, but regretted very much that it could offer no light on the situation.

Ram Singh's search of East Indian groups had been equally unsuccessful. There was no reason, of course, that the killer must be a Hindu worshipper of the six-armed goddess of destruction. Any strong man could master that murder trick.

Finally, Wentworth looked up wearily from the papers and smiled into the intent eyes of his servant.

"Well done, O Ram Singh," he said "Your reports are very thorough."

THE HINDU bowed with his cupped hands to his forehead, pride on his stern, high-cheeked countenance. Ram Singh was from the northern provinces of India, the hill country whence powerful fighters sprang. He had fought Afghans with the knife, and won.

"I have a feeling," Wentworth told his servant briefly, "that the crisis of this battle is near. So far, every battle has gone to the enemy. I have eliminated a few, but they were underlings and the enemy constantly increases in power. Arrange a lunch for me now; have the Northrup ready for two o'clock. Then hold yourself ready to receive orders by radio from me at any time. The messages will be in Hindustani."

Ram Singh's face showed disappointment.

"I know," Ram Singh," Wentworth continued softly, "that you have not wetted your knife in the battle, but the time is near." He frowned. "I feel it. The propaganda is growing too hysterical. I am sure, too, that the march of the Silver Battalions has some connection with the drive. Their leader, Simms, is far from honest. The real crisis will be here in Washington when the bills come up for passage. No, Ram Singh, you are much too valuable here for me to take you with me. I need here a strong hand that will not swerve from the death blow!"

Ram Singh's face no longer was disappointed. The light in his dark eyes, darker beneath the sweep of his white house turban, was almost fanatical, such was his attachment and worship of Wentworth.

"Han sahib!" he bowed again, cupped hands to his forehead in token of respect.

"One thing more, Ram Singh," Wentworth halted his servant as the Hindu strode toward the door. "Please call Professor Brownlee and ask him to come to Washington. I shall probably need his help."

Professor Brownlee had taught Wentworth in college and it had been in saving Brownlee from a frame-up that the Spider had been born. Now the professor used his shrewd mind in devising mechanical and chemical marvels for Wentworth. Calling him to Washington was only part of the Spider's perpetual readiness for emergencies. As yet he had no work in mind for the professor.

When Ram Singh had gone, Wentworth sat rigidly at his desk, hands flat on the blotter, staring straight before him. Never before had he felt the continual sense of impending disaster, not merely peril, but defeat! It nagged at him constantly. For a month now, he had battled this menace. His victories had been negligible. He shook his head, jerked to his feet, and paced the room. What he had told Reagh was true. Elimination of Sinclair would not halt this march of ruthless power. He must trace out the roots of this Terror and rip them from the earth!

Tonight, as a matter of caution, he would mount guard over the plane winging the Senators westward. His own Northrup, under a special government permit, carried machine guns, two firing forward through the propeller, two more twinned on a Scaarf-ring about the aft cockpit.

He took off from Anacosta Naval Field five minutes after the Senators' plane rose from Hoover airport. His plane cruised some forty miles an hour faster than the giant, twin-motored Condor of the Sinclair party, and as he circled at 15,000 feet to watch the ship, he thought swiftly over the events just before the take-off.

Sinclair had hurried to the airport, Ram Singh had reported by telephone, and said that business was detaining him at the last minute. He wanted the senators to go ahead. He would join them later by fast plane.

Wentworth heard that news with a tightening of his heart. Disaster to the plane was possible now without injury to the

Silver King himself. It was damnably suspicious, but throughout the calm sunshine of late afternoon, nothing occurred that might be construed as menacing. Ram Singh had contrived to search the plane, under pretense of looking for the luggage which Wentworth had sent to the Condor, and had found nothing that might resemble a bomb.

The low-lying sun gilded the Condor golden as it winged high over the Appalachians where the valleys were already purple with twilight. When the riding lights presently blossomed out, Wentworth swooped closer, flying dark. They were following the regular air lanes west tracing out the circling beams of the beacons, the radio signals.

At ten o'clock, Ram Singh's staccato Hindustani came over the air. The reason that Sinclair had been detained was that Tony Sinclair had picketed his foster-father's quarters in Washington and insisted on an interview. Their talk had lasted three hours. At the end of that time, the younger Sinclair had stormed from the hotel and Sinclair, senior, scowling, had made his way to a plane. He was now on the way west in a Lockheed Vega that had the edge on Wentworth's Northrup for speed. The son also was flying westward.

The Condor soared steadily on with its hidden escort. It was four hours later that death struck suddenly and without warning from a low-hanging cloud-bank.

A fast, single-seated plane burst into view two thousand feet above the Condor and streaked toward it in a screaming power-dive. Wentworth, eyes strained by long watching, did not see the ship until it had closed half the distance, then he thrust the stick forward and roared on its trail.

His mouth grim, Wentworth's thumbs hovered over the pressure trigger of his machine gun. He had guessed right. The Assassins planned to send the plane-load of irreconcilable senators crashing to a bloody death!

CHAPTER 6
A NATION AT STAKE

THE THREE planes in this high pantomime of death were picked out in black and silver. From where Wentworth bucked headwinds at ten thousand feet, the other two ships were mere gilded fireflies. Their exhausts made pale rose blotches against the black majesty of the earth.

Hard to believe, among all this ethereal beauty, that the fate of the nation rode the skies, that the tiny diving bug four thousand feet below him meant murder and destruction to the eleven men, unsuspecting aboard the Condor a thousand feet nearer earth.

Hard to believe, yes. But even as the thought flashed across Wentworth's mind he was acting. He pulled the throttle wide in a wind-trembling dive. The moan of the wind along the Northrup's fuselage rose to a shriek. He was diving at terrific speed, plunging downward more rapidly than the murder plane below, but he had at least four times the distance to cover. He could not hope to overtake it before it struck the Condor down.

Would that plane have machine guns, Wentworth wondered, or did it plan to bomb the Condor into destruction? He doubted

One of Wentworth's bullets found a vital spot. Flame leapt back from the attacking plane.

the ship mounted guns. The government allowed such weapons to few ships. If it were a bomb attack, he would gain a few minutes, but still not enough. There was a slim chance....

Kicking the nose of the Northrup to the right to clear the Condor, Wentworth pressed the triggers of his propeller guns. There was not the remotest chance that he could hit the attacker at this distance, but he might frighten the killer off; bluff him into delaying

the destruction of the Condor until he could dispose of the enemy above.

He fired a half dozen bursts into the night. Below him nothing changed. The smaller plane still rushed in viciously to murder. Wentworth tugged out a Very pistol, part of the plane's equipment, and fired the long-barreled weapon into the West ahead of the Condor. The shell burst with a vivid red glare that glinted on the backs of the planes below, that tinged the rising ridges of the hills with lurid light.

Still the small killer plane, diving to the attack, did not falter. It streaked on, straight for the Condor, perilously close now. Those two ships seemed almost within touching distance. Possibly a hundred yards still separated them, a hundred yards that would be covered in a flash of time. Wentworth cursed. He had destroyed any advantage of surprise he might have in order to warn the Condor of its impending fate, to gain a few moments' delay. And it was futile. The great biplane droned steadily on its way, its pilot and passengers unaware of the murder that darted at them from the skies.

Terrible to know that death might strike at them while he rushed futilely through space. Of what use would the Spider's vengeance be? If these eleven men died, their crash would sound the knell of the country, place it helpless in the hands of its despoilers. Frantic, while he fought to extract another notch of speed from his powerful ship, Wentworth fired another flare.

Even as he did, he saw that the pilot of the Condor had at last spotted his danger. The giant biplane had never been built for war-time maneuvers and acrobatics, but the pilot was skillful.

As the attacking plane swooped in for the kill, the Condor staggered, skated off to the left in a screaming sideslip, fairly jerked away from under the assault. The tiny wasp of death swept on, spun in a steep bank to follow. The biplane checked, slipped in the opposite direction.

Once more the killer plane was out-maneuvered. It swept past without striking, looped for position again. Wentworth shouted words that were snatched from his lips by the wind, words of encouragement, words of hope. For the killer had lost precious seconds. In moments now, Wentworth would be within striking distance. Struts and guys were shrieking with his speed. The Northrup's propeller clawed the air with full motor, bellowing to the attack like the hunting roar of some incredible beast of prey. As he dived in, Wentworth tripped the triggers of his machine guns, spewed lead into the night, streaked the black of the sky with the firefly sparks of tracer bullets. Possibly he could scare off the killer now, though he still was too far away for effective fire.

With a curse that rasped in his throat he saw that the killer recognized the firing was ineffective. Instead of turning from his attack on the Condor, instead of whirling into battle against the ship above, the Assassin plane streaked once more at the craft that carried the Senators, that bore the fate of the nation. Another side-slip would not elude him now. He would be ready for it. On he darted, closer, closer. Wentworth's mouth jerked open as if to cry warning.

Abruptly the Condor dived, jerked its nose straight down in a vertical plunge. Its tail whipped from side to side as the pilot kicked the rudder. Dangerous business, that dive. It was racking horribly the giant biplane with its one hundred fifty feet of wing spread, but once more the attack ship was out-maneuvered. Like an angry wasp, it swept up, poised as if undecided which of its enemies to attack. Wentworth was positive now that the ship carried no machine guns. At least three times the big transport had been across its prow and there had been no flicker of death fire behind the killer's propeller.

LIFE SEEMED to stand still for an instant while the killer's ship hovered between attack and defense. High up in the night sky, written only in the bellow of powerful motors, men were battling for the fate of the nation, three men in different planes, the pilot of the giant Condor, the murderous killer in his speedy single-seater, Wentworth in his roaring Northrup. If the Condor crashed, nothing on earth could prevent the Silver Assassins from seizing control of Congress, from battering through bill after bill that would distort the currency of the nation to their own personal advantage. That would mean ruin to the people.

The fate of the nation rested on the accuracy of Wentworth's gunfire, on the skill of the Condor's pilot. But now, at last, the Northrup was within striking distance. Zooming to bring his guns above the level of the Senators' plane, Wentworth sent his tracers feeling for the killer. The small plane flipped upward, whirled and zipped toward the Northrup. Abruptly flame danced behind its whining propeller. Wentworth swore in amazement. The ship did have machine guns!

Wentworth threw his plane into an Immelmann, then into a slow loop while the killer hammered by below him. He understood abruptly why the Assassin had not used its guns on the

Condor. The crash of the passenger ship must seem an accident and there would be no time to gouge machine gun bullets from the bodies of the Senators and their pilots!

Coming out of the loop, Wentworth roared in pursuit. The smaller ship zoomed, swept up over his head. The Northrup skated into a similar maneuver and Wentworth cursed. His greater power was a handicap. The smaller ship could pivot on a narrower arc, cut across his own wide whirl and rip bullets into his fuselage. Even as he spotted the danger, the killer brought his guns to bear.

The situation was desperate. Had he won the first maneuver in this wild game of death in the sky only to die when hope seemed to breathe again? He had forced the Assassin to turn and fight. He was learning the killer had courage and skill—and teeth. But Wentworth fought not for himself alone. If he fell, the speedy killer could swiftly overtake the Condor again and at their second meeting there would be no champion of humanity in the skies!

Desperately Wentworth barrel-rolled, pulled back the stick while he flew upside down. He came out of the maneuver right side up and racing below the killer but headed in the opposite direction. His hand flew to the twin guns on the Scaarf-ring and he spilled lead upward into the belly of the Assassin plane. Their contact did not last a heart beat. Two planes bellowing at a combined speed of four hundred miles an hour passed each other with a burst of sound, a few bullets pecked at the belly of the upper craft, then they were past.

Wentworth Immelmanned again, found the killer had spun

about and was headed nose-on for him! They were within fifty yards of each other, roaring with the full pull of giant engines. The machine guns of both crafts hammered, but the solid metal of their motors formed perfect shields for the men.

Abruptly, Wentworth understood the reason for this mad attack. A ringer of flame pushed up from the other ship, whipped back toward the cockpit. One of his thinly sprinkled bullets had found a vital spot! Even as he discovered that, Wentworth sensed rather than heard his own motor stutter, felt it falter as he whirled violently to the right and, banking sharply, swished past the other ship so closely that their wing-tips nearly brushed.

He twisted about in his seat, staring at the other ship. The battle was over. That finger of flame had grown to a vast, bellowing envelope that sheathed the entire fuselage. The killer plane was spinning downward, its tail streaking the night sky with a spiral of flame. A hot gush of oil caught Wentworth on the back of the neck. He whirled, ducking, to his own instrument-board. A glance at the oil-gauge told him the story. In that last desperate attack, the Assassin had cut a pressure-line.

With a curse, Wentworth cut his motor, swung in a wide, powerless circle. In the sudden silence of the engine, the rush and whisper of the wind became audible. A glance ahead showed that the giant Condor, rising against the moon, was soaring into the West, a silver ship against a silvery sky. For the present, those men were safe, but Death reached its bony hand into the clouds. The Northrup was swooping downward into the blackness of a desolate hill country. On every side trees were thick; mountains showed precipitate walls. The night cried, "Death to the Spider!"

Far below, the plunging plane of the killer struck the edge of a precipice, scattering gouts of flame; then it tumbled down the face of the cliff, blasted into fragments as it hit bottom. Wentworth heard the dull boom of the explosion drift up toward him. The circling, descending Northrop shuddered slightly in the vibration of the air.

Wentworth was studying the earth below without hope. Not a chance of a safe landing. He would have to abandon the Northrup, use a parachute. Every moment he delayed made the leap itself more dangerous. Yet he knew that, he was miles from any town in a desolate district of jumbled mountains. It might take him days to reach civilization again, days in which the Assassins might sweep the country unchecked. He could only hope that the Senators would send a search party... But there was no choice....

WENTWORTH SPOTTED a break in the thick growth of trees below him, leveled off the plane and jumped in the whining slipstream. A few breaths after he jerked the rip-cord of his parachute, the tops of the trees flashed past. He caught a glimpse of a white shelter tent, of picketed horses, then spilled to earth in a small clearing. He sprang up alertly, a smile on his lips. He had run into luck. He could buy a horse, race to the nearest town. Already three men were running toward him.

Wentworth began to unbuckle his parachute rapidly. One of the men sprang at him. Wentworth's eyes flew wide. He ducked, but so sudden and unexpected was the attack that a violent blow caught him in the face. He reeled backward, his feet caught in the 'chute shrouds and he pitched to the ground. The man kicked him in the ribs twice before the other two hauled him off.

Wentworth thrust up dazedly from the earth and gazed into the muzzles of revolvers. One of the men, taller than the other two, snatched Wentworth's gun from its holster.

"You'll have to pardon the kid," the man drawled. "You shot down his brother and he was kind of upset about it."

His brother—the brother of the killer-pilot! That meant, then, that these men were allies of the Silver Assassins, that he had fallen into the hands of his enemies, miles from any help, from any possibility of escape. He had won aloft, but he was a helpless captive now. The Assassins' conspiracy would reign supreme. Wentworth struggled up, hands going again to the harness.

"Just leave that there parachute strapped on," the leader drawled. "It'll make is easier to keep track of you until we find out what Sinclair wants us to do."

The words confirmed all Wentworth's fears. He was in the hands of the enemy. "Sinclair, hell!" snarled the man who had attacked Wentworth. "This man's my prisoner and I'm going to burn him the way he burned Roy."

WENTWORTH STARED at the three men, their faces shadowed by wide brimmed hats, at their leveled heavy revolvers. Truly, the ramifications of the Assassins' organization were wide. Apparently, these men had been placed here to make sure that when the Condor crashed with its human freight, that no traces of its means of destruction should be found. Sinclair planned well.

If he had needed further proof of the man's complicity in the conspiracy, this angry boy's shout would have confirmed it. Wentworth lifted a slow hand to his lip, cut by the cowardly blow, and felt that it was swelling. Luckily, he was in disguise as always now when he went upon the Spider's crusades.

Wentworth looked at the men steadily. "I thought burning at the stake was an old Spanish custom," he said. "When was it introduced here?"

For an instant the three men stared at him, then two of them broke into heavy guffaws.

"Lord," one said finally, "don't you mind Rob here. He's a little funny sometimes, but there ain't gonna be no burning at no stake, unless Sinclair orders it."

Rob cursed wildly, but he was thrust off toward the tent and the other two men bound Wentworth's hands behind him and took turns guarding him through the rest of the night. Wentworth lay awake for a long while, analyzing his chances. He thought he would have no trouble slipping his bonds after working an hour or so, even though the tool kit he carried always strapped beneath his arm was out of reach. But he doubted the advisability of escape at present.

He was miles from any town. He did not know the country, did not know what cities were near. Better, he decided finally, to remain a prisoner, to allow these men to take him to some spot where he could more readily find his way back to civilization and the battle with the Assassins; better to attempt to learn the conspirators' further plans by being taken to their headquarters.

Once he made his decision, Wentworth composed his mind and slept.

Once during the night he awoke. He was just in time to dodge an attempt by the man Rob to drive a knife through his throat. Before the youth could strike again, one of his friends knocked him down with a gun. Wentworth glared up at the guard.

"You're a hell of a watchman," he growled. "How the devil can I sleep, if you don't protect me from that damned Spanish custom?"

The flicker of the firelight showed the man was grinning.

"You're a cool hombre," he said. "Go ahead and get your shut-eye. I'll tie up the kid."

He dragged Rob to a tree. Wentworth rolled over. The guard had failed to spot the boy's knife embedded in the earth beside his head. Wentworth tugged it loose with his teeth, managed to drop it down inside his shirt. A small smile twitched his lips as he settled himself for sleep again.

They were moving at daylight. Wentworth mounted double on a horse with one of the men. When evening fell they entered a small town, but delayed only to back a car from a garage. Rob's usefulness became apparent now. He took the wheel and sent the auto bounding over a rutty hill road at breakneck speed. It was dawn when they reached a mining camp and Wentworth, still bound, was imprisoned in a cabin. He was sure that he was in the Assassins' camp, but he still had no inkling of further plans. Although he could have slashed his bonds with the knife, he decided to wait. He dropped on a bunk and slept till evening.

It was dark when a man with an oil lantern swinging in his hand thrust into the cabin and grinned at Wentworth. It was the gaunt guard who had saved him from Rob two nights before.

"Up and at 'em, hombre," the man said. "The chief is here and craves conversation with you."

Wentworth swung his feet to the floor, lurched erect. His wrists were lashed together behind his back. He grinned, too. A two-day stubble of beard assisted his disguise.

"Lead on, MacDuff," he grunted. The guard caught one of his arms and led him across a narrow street between six cabins to a large log house at the end of the lane. He thrust open the door, shoved Wentworth in first and followed, still clinging to his arm.

The cabin was a single, long, low room. At its head a heavy table had been placed and behind it sat a massive man with a comfortable grin upon his face. He had a mane of silvery hair. "Good evening, Spider," the man said.

Wentworth bowed as suavely as bound arms would permit. "Good evening, Sinclair," he said.

HE WONDERED at the daring of this man, this fabulous capitalist who stooped to crime, thus exposing and identifying himself to the men who killed for him. There was a frown in Wentworth's eyes. It seemed ridiculous and futile—incredible, in fact. Why should a man of his prominence thus expose himself to blackmail and death? Was it because he knew that soon he would be so completely in control of the nation and its affairs that he would have no reason to worry? Or was it simply that he enjoyed criminality?

"I suppose you know," Wentworth said casually, "that I am going to kill you, Sinclair?"

The grin tightened on the heavy face of the Silver King. "No," he said softly, "I didn't know that, Spider. I do know this—you will die tonight. You keep poking that infernally long nose of yours into my business and so I shall have to remove your power to poke. Get it?"

"I get it," Wentworth said dryly. "And when does this event take place?"

Outwardly he was calm. He had expected this, of course, but the definite statement sent the blood thumping in his throat, made an old thin scar upon his right temple throb. But now that he was face to face with this man, he must learn his plans.

"Tonight," said Sinclair. "Tonight you die."

Wentworth nodded. "Glad to see that you're still afraid of me," he said. "It must be that things are not working out entirely to your satisfaction. Otherwise, you wouldn't bother with me."

Sinclair's smile turned grim, his lips thinning nastily. "You think that, do you?" he asked gently.

Wentworth lifted his eyebrows. His disguise had not altered their mockery. He taunted Sinclair with a faint smile. Sinclair thumped the heavy table with his fist and the jar of the blow quivered in the boards of the floor.

"After tonight," Sinclair said violently, "I shall rule the country." The same slightly oracular tone that was typical of his foster-son, Tony, crept into his voice. "After tonight, the government shall bow to my wishes. If the President opposes me," he swept the air with his hand in a cutting motion, "that, too, can be taken care of."

"After tonight," Wentworth repeated softly. "Then you must indeed consider me very important. After you have accomplished my death, you will be supreme. But unless you kill me, all your triumphs will be empty."

Sinclair snorted. He reared to his feet, a massive, powerful man with a formidable chest. "Conceited ass," he spluttered. "You are a mere incident. Tonight, your senatorial friends die." He drew a thin watch from his pocket and glanced at it. "In precisely four hours, they die, and their death will give me complete control. I own—" he gloated over that word of possession. "I *own* a majority, a big majority, in both houses of Congress."

Wentworth felt a thrill of hope at Sinclair's words. The Senators were still alive, then! Obviously, the defeat of his attempt to kill the men in the air had necessitated a complete recasting of his plans. He had not yet struck them, would not strike for four hours. Now he knew Sinclair's intentions. If he could escape... He felt the pressure of the knife blade against his side where he had worked it beneath his belt on the left side. That was his only hope.

Sinclair was smiling at him mockingly now, lids half lowered over piercing eyes. "Four hours from now?" he said softly. "Does that give you hope, Spider? You'll escape, you think. You'll dash to the rescue. No, no, my boy. You have poked your nose into my business for the last time. For an hour, you shall sit under guard here in this room, an hour until Rob comes back from an errand on which I have sent him. Then you shall be turned over to Rob for execution."

Wentworth's hopes congealed in his heart. Under guard for an hour. Unless that guard were careless, he stood small chance of maneuvering the knife into a position where he could use it. Once Rob seized him, he stood no chance at all, and if he died the Senators would perish, all the nation would lie within the power of this fiend. His eyes glittered darkly with ugly cold lights. Sinclair read them correctly. He threw back his head and laughed, laughed until the room rang with it. "Poor, poor Spider," he choked. "I'm *so* sorry for you."

CHAPTER 7
DEATH BY TORTURE

NONE OF his despair, no emotion save amusement, showed on Wentworth's lean, resolute face. If Sinclair plotted to destroy the Senators, either they had not suspected the Silver King of complicity in the airplane attack, or he had succeeded in convincing them that he was not involved. Otherwise, he would not be able to strike at them. For by now they would have surrounded themselves with an impregnable guard.

Sinclair moved across the room—with the suave strength he always displayed. "I must be going," he crooned. "Keep the Spider under guard for an hour, then turn him over to Rob. I don't care what method Rob employs so long as he kills him."

The gaunt man who had taken Wentworth prisoner still stood just behind Wentworth, one of his hands on his bound arm. "Looky here, chief," he said in a slow drawling voice. "This Rob is clean off his nut. He wants to burn this here guy alive."

Sinclair looked startled a moment, then shrugged. "It's a bit drastic," he said. "However, let us not forget his brother died that way."

"You mean," asked the man incredulously, "that you're a-goin' to let him do it?"

A grim smile crossed Sinclair's heavy face. "Of course," he said, "if you'd like to relieve Rob of his duty, it will be all right. But there must be no bungling."

Wentworth, listening while his mind raced, felt the hand leave his arm. "I ain't aimin' to commit murder," the man growled.

Sinclair said dryly, "I thought not. However, Rob has no such scruples. I tell you what you do. Lock Rob and Wentworth in a cabin together. Rob can hardly burn him alive then without burning himself up also."

"Thanks even for small favors," Wentworth said amiably. "Would you mind telling me just why you refrained from publishing your proof that I was the Spider?"

A brief frown touched Sinclair's forehead. He opened his mouth, but did not speak. Then he waved his hand abruptly and strode by Wentworth toward the door, glancing up as he strode past. Wentworth had a momentary impression that the man was shorter than when last he had faced him in the study of his Chicago mansion, but realized that Sinclair walked with his head thrust forward. It occurred to him that not once had Sinclair addressed him as Wentworth and for a moment he wondered why.

"Remember," Sinclair called from the doorway. "Guard him constantly for an hour, then turn him over to Rob." He glanced again at his thin platinum watch. Wentworth swung about to face him, met his sardonic grin. "Sorry to leave you before the last minute," he said, "but I must hasten and dress for my appointment with the Senators. It would be a shame to keep them waiting." He pushed out into the night and the door closed hollowly.

Wentworth's lanky guard thrust him toward a stiff-backed chair. "You set there until it's time to turn you over to Rob," he said. He stared at his prisoner contemplatively, a tall man with a dour, sour-mouthed face.

Wentworth smiled at him. "I assure you I appreciate what you did," he said.

The man kept looking at him. "That's swell," he growled, "but don't get any idea in your head that I'm letting you escape. You try it and I'll forget I don't want to kill you, see?"

Wentworth said slowly, "I see."

The man meant what he said. And during the hours of wading for Rob, Wentworth feared to attempt even the loosening of the knife beneath his belt. If it were spotted and taken from him, his meager chances became even slimmer.

His hour of grace tripped by on dancing feet, was gone while his mind still mulled over abortive attempts at escape. Finally, galloping hoofbeats pounded up to the cabins and the dour guard grinned acidly.

"That'll be Rob," he said. "On time."

HE STOOD by the door, motioned Wentworth to approach,

With a rolling wrench of his body, Wentworth snapped his

arm from behind him and drove the knife at Rob.

103

then caught him tightly by the arm. As they walked out into the open, three men, shadowy figures, straightened from where they squatted about a small fire. A fourth stole forward eagerly, and Wentworth identified Rob's bunchy figure.

"I got the stake ready and the wood piled," he said like a mother announcing to her children that there was cake and ice cream for supper.

That's tough," growled the guard. "You ain't a-goin' to use them."

Rob's shoulders hunched. "Listen," he snarled "Sinclair said I could do what I wanted."

The guard nodded.

"Then, what the hell…?" Rob began.

"Anything, yeah," said the guard, "but it's got to be inside a cabin so we can take care of anything that slips."

"But I can't burn him in there!" Rob howled.

Wentworth felt strangely detached, as if this were some other person who was being threatened with death by torture. This young fiend would devise some horrible means of death, and he had only that awkward knife. He could not even shift it about his body now, when death was so close. That powerful hand still clamped on his arm. A mad impulse to tear himself loose and run for it tugged at Wentworth's mind, but even as he considered it, he knew the futility of any such effort.

Even if he were not shot down in the first ten paces, he would be helpless to escape from this wild district. No, his best chance was to go into the cabin with Rob and hope against hope that he would be able to hold off death until he could free himself.

He would still be a prisoner in the camp, but at least the danger from Rob would be removed. Each inch gained along the road to safety, along the road to freeing the nation of the curse of the Silver Assassins, must mean the conquering of impossible odds. But if he succeeded in this first step, the others might become easier....

The guard finally convinced Rob that he quoted Sinclair literally and Wentworth was thrust toward a small cabin with Rob running eagerly ahead. He lighted a lantern and the grotesque shadows of his bunchy figure were like a crouching grant upon the wall. The guard thrust Wentworth into the cabin and Rob slammed the door, turned his pinched, maniacal face upon his prisoner.

He knocked Wentworth down with a kick in the stomach, slammed his boot three times into his ribs. Wentworth writhed, his muscles quivering with pain despite his sternest efforts, but not a sound escaped him. He struck suddenly at Rob with both feet but his torturer danced out of the way. He tossed a loop about Wentworth's feet, suspended them from a rafter so his captive's weight rested on his shoulder blades.

"That was just a taste of what's to come," Rob whispered, gloating. "I'm so glad you can take it. I'm so glad. I was afraid you'd faint on me and couldn't get the full pleasure out of what I'm planning for you."

With Wentworth dangling helpless, Rob crossed to the stove and built a fire. He thrust an iron poker into it to heat. He came back and began kicking Wentworth again so that his half-suspended body swayed in the rope. It hurt like hell.

"Get the idea, louse?" Rob panted hoarsely. "I can't burn you alive, so I'm going to heat that poker until its white hot and then I'm going to let it burn its way right through your guts. You'll live a while, louse, quite a while."

Wentworth twisted from the blows of the man's boots. They were an agony against his sides despite the strength of his superb muscles. His mind was dazed with the pain of the attack, combined with the hour of muddling over the hopelessness of his attempted escape. But even as he twisted, a slow plan began to form in Wentworth's mind. He writhed about so that the boots struck upon the knife.

The edge bit into his flesh. His head flung back; his breath hissed between his teeth. He felt blood flow warmly from the gash. Rob drew back his boot again, then held it there poised.

"Hell," the madman muttered disgustedly. "You're soft. If I'm not careful you'll die before I get the poker hot."

The boot came harmlessly down to the floor. Rob deliberately turned his back and crossed to the stove, began to rattle the lid and tinker with the draft-regulator. Wentworth relaxed slowly, glancing down at his side. The blood staining his clothes had led his torturer to believe he was badly injured, that his side had been kicked in.

A THIN-LIPPED grin distorted Wentworth's mouth. In stopping the torture, his trick had achieved more than he had dared hope. For he also had accomplished his primary purpose. That kick which had rasped the naked blade against his side had jarred the knife nearly loose from the binding of his belt! Now it was almost free. He shot a quick look at Rob. The man's back was still turned. He pulled out the poker, growled because it was only a dull red, and thrust it back into the fire again.

Wentworth tightened the rigid muscles of his abdomen so that his stomach no longer pressed tautly against the belt, so that the knife lay loose against his body. Then he pressed upward with his feet on the rope that strained them toward the rafters. It lifted the lower part of his body still higher so that the knife, of its own weight, slid completely free. It now lay loosely beneath his shirt. A slight twist of his body and it snaked along his side and was in the back where his bound hands could fumble it through the thickness of his flannel shirt.

Rob spun around abruptly, staring at Wentworth with maddened, suspicious eyes. But his captive lay limply in the bight of the rope, his shoulder-blades rubbing the floor, eyes closed.

"I'll have something to wake you up in a moment my friend," Rob grunted harshly. He strode over, tapped tentatively on Wentworth's jaw with his boot-toe. It jarred the Spider's whole brain. Abruptly Rob straddled his body, dropped heavily to a seat upon his stomach. His hands flew to Wentworth's face. He pushed dirty thumbnails down beside his prisoner's nose, jabbing painfully at the eyes. He increased the pressure gradually, thumbs sinking deeper and deeper, gouging. The purpose was to squeeze the entire eyeball from the socket. The pain was clear agony.

Wentworth would have to work fast. Blindness and death crowded in upon him. His mind was half-dazed with suffering. He had manipulated the point of the knife so that it was against the fabric of his shirt. With a swift push, he made it cut through the cloth and now he gripped the naked blade with his hands. The pain of his eyes was incredible. Blinding white lights shot against his brain. Rob put on more pressure. Wentworth locked his teeth in his lip to choke down the gasp of pain. His lip bled.

He writhed under the torture, tossing his body, pressing his feet upward into the sling. The exquisite agony of his eyes was enough to make him scream aloud; it sent quivering nausea through his stomach, but that was not the reason Wentworth squirmed. He was manipulating his arms, bound beneath him, held down by his own and his captor's weight. After intolerable minutes of the eye-torture, Wentworth got the knife against the cords.

He was half mad with the pain of his eyes now. He wrenched his head violently from side to side to escape those fearful thumbs. Then abruptly, the ropes parted on his wrists. He was free!… Well, say one-tenth free. His hands were able to move, now, but they were numb from the ropes. His feet were still bound above his head. This man sat terribly upon his body and tormented him. Outside a ring of armed men waited… but Wentworth had gained an inch of the way toward freedom, an inch—and he had a weapon!

WITH A rolling wrench of his body, Wentworth seized the knife by the handle, snapped his arm from beneath him and drove the blade straight at Rob's throat. But Wentworth's arms were numb. They had been bound for many hours. His grasp on the knife was weak.

With a shout, Rob tumbled from his seat. The knife gashed

his out-thrown arm, but did not gouge it deeply. Rob staggered to his feet, snatching at his gun.

Wentworth was still helpless to rise; his feet were roped to the rafters. He had freed his hands. He had a feeble weapon, but Rob, with a sneer on his face, had a gun in his hand now. Good God! After this hopeless struggle against odds, was he to die now that he had won an inch of the way to freedom? Was he to die and drag the nation down to its doom with him?

"Drop that knife," Rob snarled, "or I'll smash your arm with a bullet. I'd rather not because you can suffer more from the poker if you ain't hurt much otherwise, but—*drop that knife!*"

Straining his aching, throbbing eyes, Wentworth saw that Rob crouched, back close to the stove, the black mouth of his forty-five leveled at him. His fingers fumbled the knife blade with only dull feeling. Restoring circulation sent agonies of pain-through his hands and arms.

"You've got till I count three," Rob snapped. "If you ain't dropped the knife by then, I'm goin' to smash that arm!"

Wentworth let the knife lie flat on the palm of his hand. Gathering his strength, he ripped a horrid scream from his throat and in the same instant, hurled the knife with a twist of his body that put all his weight and strength into the throw. It glinted in the dim light of the cabin like a streak of silver. Rob flinched at the scream as he had been intended to. His gun blasted. A cry bubbled in his throat and stopped in a gasp.

Wentworth's throbbing eyes described that in the fluster of fast action, Rob had fired not at his prisoner, but at the flying knife! He saw that the knife was buried to the hilt in Rob's throat. The gun clattered to the floor. The man plucked at the knife weakly, spun, and fell against the stove where the torture iron still heated.

Wentworth's whole body was racked with the pain of the blows he had suffered, his eyes throbbed and ached, but for him there could be no moment's surcease, no rest. He doubled forward toward his feet, fumbled the knots with deadened fingers. It took him five minutes to loosen the ropes and during that time, his straining ears kept watch. Not a sound came from outside the cabin. If the men had heard the cries, they had taken them for the suffering of the prisoner.

A grim smile of triumph twisted Wentworth's mouth as the last knot came free and he struggled to his feet. He became abruptly aware of a nauseous stench in the cabin, the smell of singed hair and scorched human flesh! He turned toward Rob, dead from the knife he had used not many hours before in an attempt to kill Wentworth. Spiraling smoke sizzled from the man's face, resting against the reddening belly of the stove. Wentworth caught his feet and dragged him clear, rolled him over on his back.

For a moment Wentworth was staggered at what he saw. He turned his face away and an uncontrollable shudder shook his body. He reeled on faltering feet across the room to where a bucket of water stood. He ignored a tin dipper and tilted the entire bucket to his mouth, spilled the balance over his head and body. He gasped at the bite of its coldness, then stood panting. He shook his head violently, then forced himself back to the body. He kept his face partially averted and deliberately began to strip the clothes from Rob, replacing them with his own.

Wentworth drove himself to the task. Within five minutes, he was ready to leave. Rob's gun was tied low on his thigh, and Rob's clothing, a little tight for him, but not noticeably small, was upon him. He did not take the time to disguise his features into the likeness of Rob. Within a couple of hours the Senators would die! He dragged Rob's hat low over his forehead, walked with Rob's slight shoulder-rocking swagger to the door, and jerked it open.

The tall guard who had turned Wentworth over to the madman for execution stepped from the shadows. "Finished?" he asked gently.

"Yeah," Wentworth made his voice thick, as if he were glutted with blood-lust, "yeah, but the mugg couldn't take it. He died too fast."

The guard looked into the cabin and cursed in a low frightened voice. He turned away, reeling. "You damned bloody fiend!" he said hoarsely. "You *fiend!*"

Wentworth laughed coarsely. "What's the matter? Can't you take it, either?" He swaggered after the guard, watched him stonily as the man leaned against a tree and retched.

WENTWORTH'S BACK was turned toward the flicker of the camp fire, his face shadowed by the dragged down brim of Rob's wide Stetson. None of the other three men who sauntered up looked further than his clothes. Why should they? Rob had been placed in a cabin with a helpless man and told to kill that man. He had been aching to do just that thing! Why should they suspect that the faceless corpse in there was Rob and this man of whom they were all slightly afraid now was the helpless prisoner?

Presently the lanky guard straightened and walked unsteadily toward where horses moved uneasily in the darkness, shaking their heads with a jangling of bits. A pony nickered and the sound seemed uncertain, fraught with fear. Wentworth trailed the others toward the horses. He had no time to lose. He must escape these men and fly to the rescue of the Senators—a race with murder.

Within four hours—approximately midnight, Sinclair had said—the Senators were to die. How long had he been in the hands of the guards since then? He had waited an hour with the lanky watcher, then he had been turned over to Rob. But that torture had been short for all that the ache and torment of his body still sent waves of heat-like pain over him. Say, half an hour. Two hours and a half before Sinclair would strike at the Senators, the only men who stood between him and complete domination of the country. But where were the Senators, and what was the nature of the attack? Where was Sinclair?

Wentworth knew none of the answers to these questions and he rode the dark mountain roads with four men who were servants of Sinclair even to the point of murder!

As they rode single file through the close-growing trees, Wentworth bringing up the rear, he noticed that one of the men ahead was dropping back toward him. Except to watch the man as closely as possible in the darkness of the overshadowing trees, Wentworth did nothing. There was nothing he could do that would not excite suspicion. He slowed his horse and, without warning, a blaze of white light dazzled his eyes. The man who had been dropping back toward him cursed violently, snapped a warning order.

"You're covered, don't try any tricks, Mr. Spider!" he barked.

The other riders whirled back, along the narrow trail. "I didn't think he sat his horse like Rob," the man with the light explained rapidly, "then I got to thinking about that guy back in the cabin not having a face…."

His sentence broke off with a curse, for Wentworth, kicking suddenly free of his stirrups, pitched to the ground on the far side of his horse. As he threw himself deliberately into the cover of his mount's body, he snatched his gun from its holster and blazed away under the pony's neck. Three times he shot and the flashlight flew upward. Its beam made slashing circles in the darkness. The white ray flashed over the man who had held the light and showed him toppling to the earth with his mouth wide in the surprise of death. The beam spotted a second man slumped limply on the neck of his horse. Hoofbeats pounded up the trail and Wentworth emptied his gun after the surviving two of those who had guarded him. They did not even return the fire, but fled in haste.

Examining of the bodies, printing on the foreheads of the two he had slain the mocking red seal of the Spider, Wentworth was fleetingly glad that the gaunt guard who had saved him from death by fire was not among those he had killed. Leaving the dead behind, Wentworth spurred on along the trail. He was free, but save that he knew he was in the mountains, he had no definite idea of his whereabouts. A glance at the stars showed him the trail led eastward. As he topped a notch in the ridge, with the hoofbeats of the other rider faint in the distance, the moon slid over the horizon and threw black shadows and silver light over a jumble of hills, of gashed canyons, and up-flung peaks.

Wentworth pulled his mount to a halt and swept the horizon. Off in the northeast, he made out the faint loom of a crag. He stared at it with straining, aching eyes. Then he smiled. Pike's Peak. He knew where he was now. If he pushed due east for five or six miles, he would hit the automobile road that linked Colorado Springs with Denver. He clapped spurs in and set the horse at a hard gallop down the trail.

BUT WENTWORTH was soon forced to slow his pace because of uncertain footing. Deep and precipitate gullies forced detours and it was an hour and a half before he reached the white concrete strip of the road. An hour before Sinclair struck, one hour and he still had no idea at all where the Senators were or what the blow would be. One thing he knew, the blow meant death to the Senators, it meant the doom of the country, thrown into the unscrupulous control of a murdering, thieving gang of assassins.

He put the horse at a full gallop up the soft strip beside the concrete, scanning the road eagerly for glimpse of an automobile. A glimmer of lights revealed a gasoline station. Wentworth swung stiffly from the saddle, clumped with a rider's stiff-kneed stride into the building and got hold of a phone. The attendant grinned at him.

"First time I ever heard of a hoss comin' to a gas station," he said.

"Trade him to you, even, for that wreck of a motorcycle you've got," Wentworth offered. Then his call went through. Yes, said the New Era hotel-clerk, Miss Van Sloan was registered there, but she was out at present. Wentworth made a second call.

"Rocky Mountain News," a man's voice said wearily.

Wentworth got hold of the city editor. "Listen," he said, voice blurred as if with drink. "This is Armstrong of the New York World. Where in hell are those Senators? I slide out for a drink, and when I come back, they've gone places. Wonder they wouldn't let a fellow know."

The editor's voice laughed at him. "Did you say *a drink?*" he wondered. "They've gone out to the Yellow Hornet shaft for dinner."

Wentworth guffawed. "Gonna eat nuggets?"

"Nope," the editor was sneering now. "Sinclair mined a solid block of silver—weighs over a half a ton—down on the thirteenth level. They're using that for a table and they say it's some party."

"Criminee!" Wentworth wailed. "And me missing out on that? So long, I'll be seeing you!"

Wentworth spun toward the garage man to find him staring at him with suspicious eyes, a gun steady in his right hand.

"You ain't no newspaper man," he said curtly. "And I aim to find out just what you're up to before you stir out of this dump."

Wentworth cursed. "Don't be a fool," he said. "I'm a government agent and I've got to get to the Senators."

115

The man grinned coldly. "Last man came out here saying he was a government agent turned out to be the Spider," he said. "How come if you're a government man you don't know where the Senators are? Nope, it don't hold water."

Wentworth was raging with impatience. The Yellow Hornet shaft was twenty miles from here and five of that was over a road that an automobile would have a hell of a time negotiating at more than five miles an hour. If he made the best possible time, it would take him nearly forty minutes to reach the scene of the plotted murders. And when he reached there, he still would be utterly in the dark as to what form the attack would take. He had not a minute to lose.

"Listen," he argued with the garage man, "I haven't got time to argue with you about this, but the Senators are due to be attacked in an hour. I've got to get there and help them."

The garage man was circling warily now, pushing Wentworth away from the phone with the leveled gun. He was grinning knowingly.

"Sure, sure," he said, "and President Roosevelt is going to be assassinated tomorrow. And you're the only man that can save him." He reached the phone, asked for the sheriff's office. "You're going to stay right here, buddy, until the sheriff has the time to look over your papers. And don't get nervous. I'm a deputy myself and a prime shot with a six-gun."

"Damn it, man," Wentworth's anger crept into his voice. "The fate of the…."

He choked it off. Such words were futile. The man, no one, would accept the truth as anything except a stupendous tale concocted in an effort to free himself. Who, among the people of the country, would believe that the next hour would decide the fate of the nation?

Wentworth sprang forward and the garage man's gun spat flame and lead. A bullet plucked at the Stetson on Wentworth's head. He jerked to a halt, still an impossible distance from the man with the gun. He could not attack without taking a bullet in his body that would put him hopelessly out of the fight, that would be tantamount to dooming the country. Yet there was only a brief time in which he could act. At least five minutes of that precious hour had already flown....

"Listen, hombre," said the garage man dryly. "Don't try that again. That shot was just for fun. Next time, I'll stop kidding!"

CHAPTER 8
RIVER OF FLAME

DEATH LOOKED at Wentworth from the deputy's eyes and he recognized that cold, implacable gaze for what it was. Even if the Spider warred on police, it would be impossible for him to draw and shoot before the other man sent deadly lead smashing into his own body. If he waited, he might hope to catch the man when his vigilance relaxed for a moment, but he could not wait. Each minute that ticked past brought the nation nearer the abyss of destruction.

That abortive charge on the leveled gun had brought Wentworth within six feet of the man, had brought him to the corner of an old-fashioned roll-top desk that held the phone. Between

117

him and the garage man was a swivel chair and on the floor beside it rested a gabboon. Wentworth's head hung as he studied these factors.

He began to move his hands, grasping the back of the chair, sliding them back and forth along the wood. The deputy watched his hands sharply, glanced at his bloodshot eyes. But Wentworth did not need his eyes for the thing he was doing. Furtively, he inserted his toe in the mouth of the cuspidor while his moving hands held the deputy's eye.

Abruptly Wentworth tossed the cuspidor into the air, directly at the deputy. At the same instant, he hurled himself forward and to the right. The man's gun blasted and glass crashed as a big window dissolved into silvery fragments. Even as the man fired, the cuspidor struck his hand, spilled filth over his body.

The deputy cursed, leaping backward to bring his gun to bear again, but it was too late. His shoulders hit the wall and Wentworth was upon him with swinging fists. His knuckles rapped nerve centers in the man's gun arm and the revolver dropped from powerless fingers. His left struck again like lightning, bouncing off the taut muscles of the deputy's stomach, then his right crashed to the jaw.

The deputy reeled and Wentworth was upon him like a tornado, raining shoulder-rocking lefts and rights to the jaw. His late captor crumpled unconscious to the floor. Wentworth whirled, breathing quickly, toward the door. No one in sight. The rasping of the dangling telephone caught his ear.

Wentworth snatched it up. "Chief!" he panted, imitating the deputy's voice, making it hoarse with breathlessness. "Couple of guys held me up, headed for Denver. Blue Lincoln sedan, Colorado plates. Didn't get number. Yeah, I'm chasing them."

He slammed up the receiver, yanked the phone wires loose, and, stopping only to snatch the garage man's gun, darted from the service station to the motorcycle he had spotted beside the building. He glanced at the fuel gauge, kicked the motor into life and zipped down the road. Fifteen miles of swift going... He wrenched the accelerator grip far over, blasted down the road at ninety miles an hour. He was crouched low between the handle-bars. The wind whipped off his hat, battered his face and pushed his breath back into his nostrils. His tortured eyes ached, ached....

That phone call would throw the officers off the trail for a while. They would put a cordon across the Denver road and he was speeding in the opposite direction. It would be probably ten minutes before the deputy recovered, then, the phone out of order, his only means of communication would be a horse. Undoubtedly, he would make tracks to the nearest phone, but by that time the sheriff should be out of reach....

Wentworth covered the fifteen miles of concrete road in a little over ten minutes. Braking with foot-stabs at the pedal, he slowed the motorcycle to a crawl and jounced into a narrow dirt road that was little more than a foot-path. The Senators undoubtedly had been flown to the scene, possibly in autogiros—there was a landing field, he knew—but he had no time to get a plane. This trail was his way. The men who worked the mine all lived around the shaft. The ore was shipped out on a long cable stretched across miles of unbroken forest. An old

A swing of the shovel smashed the wagon from which Sinclair had been speaking, hurling flying fragments after fleeing men.

shaft, the Yellow Hornet, which had yielded treasure in 'ninety-eight. Wentworth recalled its history as he bounced along. In the old days, mule trains had brought the silver and gold out as they did even now in some of the more isolated districts. For years, it had yielded a fortune in precious metals, then a blast had pierced the tunnel of an underground river which had boiled out into the drives and shafts—literally boiled, for the water had a temperature of one hundred seventy degrees!

It had been an engineering problem of extreme delicacy to dam the flood and the owners of former days had not attempted it. Now that the price of silver was soaring, thanks to the manipulation of the syndicate, the project had become worth while. The boiling river had been dammed and, under forced ventilation, the half-mile deep shaft was being worked again. Planes brought in supplies.

WENTWORTH THOUGHT these things over rapidly as his motorcycle jounced and twisted like a live thing over the bumps of the trail. In spots the pathway climbed in a jerky zig-zag up a hillside; at others it led through six-inch sand in creek bottoms. It was constant fight to keep the cycle upright, heartbreaking, nerve-racking work, but Wentworth fought on at speeds that would have spelled suicide for a less skillful operator.

A mile from the mine itself, where the mountain began to sweep up from the bottoms, Wentworth thrust the motorcycle into the underbrush and pushed on afoot. The coolness of the night helped him. He had still a half hour before the time set for the Senators' death, but it would take him at least ten minutes to reach the shaft and once there he had no key to the danger.

It would not be enough to warn the men, even assuming that they would take his word that peril threatened. He must ferret out the danger and destroy it.

Wentworth was passing the landing field now, a level valley half-way up the slope of the mountain that had been cleared of brush and trees. An unwary, footstep off to his right stopped him in his tracks. He waited, heard the step again, and wormed into the shrubbery. It might be a guard. It might be one of the conspirators, but either way it was trouble for the Spider.

Wentworth moved with his noiseless skill toward the sound of the steps, heard a muffled cry and sprang forward. An elbow chunked into his ribs, fingers twisted into his hair, and beneath his grasping arms he felt the smooth slide of silk. What the hell! *A woman!* He jerked clear, sprayed light from a pocket flashlight, then laughed softly.

"Hello, darling," he said.

The girl gasped, "Dick!"

It was Nita van Sloan. She wore riding clothes, a blouse of silk, and her chestnut curls were tumbled about her face bewitchingly. Wentworth switched off the light.

"What brought you here, sweet?" he asked.

Already he was urging her speedily on toward the Yellow Hornet shaft. There was not a second to lose.

"I followed Harry Black and Tony Sinclair out here," she said. "So far as I've been able to discover, Blade is crazy about this Bessie Kendall and Elsa is crazy about him. But Tony is giving him a run for his money with both of them. Tony seems to fancy himself as a lady killer." There was mild amusement in Nita's tones.

"I hope the—wounds won't prove fatal," Wentworth laughed appreciatively. Before this, he had seen predatory males come to grief at Nita's capable hands.

"So far," Nita murmured, "the wounds have all been verbal. But Dick, I have a hunch that something big is on tonight. Black and Tony flew here for a labor meeting. And this is one of the syndicate's biggest mines. I think the Senatorial party is coming here tonight and this demonstration is to impress them."

Wentworth pushed on rapidly, eyes narrowed in thought. Perhaps this was the plot against the Senators, perhaps a battle was to be staged and the Senators assassinated, made to appear the victims of the labor agitators. That would be clever enough to have been planned by Sinclair.

"Did Black and Tony call this meeting, or were they asked to attend?" he asked swiftly. If they had been called in, probably the meeting had been planned by the Assassins.

"Invited to attend, I think," said Nita.

Wentworth slapped his fist into his palm. "That's it, then." He told Nita rapidly then what had happened since last he had seen her, and what threatened tonight. When he had finished, they had reached the edge of a clearing where the mine cabins were built. The company was scooping a great level cut out of the mountain side as a site for the homes and a large steam shovel stood just before them.

Apparently the men had been working night as well as day, for the steam hissed idly from the shovel and mule-drawn wagons stood nearby. Fifty feet beyond the steam-shovel a group of a hundred men was congregated. Standing on a wagon, the short, dynamic figure of Tony Sinclair bellowed sonorous phrases.

The men had formed a dense semi-circle about Sinclair and they effectually blocked any entrance to the mine. The shaft itself was remote against the hillside, cut in at the foot of a fifty-foot precipice which protected it completely on one side. The structure above the shaft was gaily decorated with bunting and oil flares.

Wentworth strained his ears to hear what Tony had to say. He caught only snatches on the flaws of the wind. "… bloody capitalists… selfish bosses… iron heel of tyranny.…"

OBVIOUSLY THE usual sort of Communistic cant. The men were talking it good-humoredly, laughing and jeering at Tony. Some few were with him, but they were a minority. These were well paid workers on a whole. Many of them had been idle for months, even years, but they had jobs now and three meals a day. It would be hard to arouse them to the point where the murder of the Senators could be accomplished.

Wentworth starred uneasily. Not more than ten minutes now to the time set for the murder. Suppose his theory of the method to be used were wrong?

"Stay here, darling," he murmured and drifted toward the crowd. A man stepped from the shadows.

"Where are you going, hombre?" he asked softly.

"Just going to listen to that guy rave," Wentworth replied good-humoredly. He was quite close to the man now and the fellow started.

"You don't belong here," he snapped. "What the hell…?"

Wentworth's left looped to his chin and the man sprawled into the underbrush. A quick glance showed that the crowd had not been disturbed by this exchange in the shadows. He pushed on, mingled with the crowd. Abruptly, something brushed across the back of his head, a numbing blow caught his arm. He ducked; whirled, and lanced out with his fist. A man fell but in two seconds, a half dozen men were charging in from all sides. Guards darted from the underbrush in a score of places.

With two swift blows, Wentworth knocked down two men. He ducked backward then, buried himself into the crowd. Everywhere about him tumult reigned. Men shouted and Tony Sinclair's bellowed epithets beat upon them futilely. Wentworth worked his way to the edge of the battling mob, darted to the shadows of the trees. He stared out over the fighters. Behind the speaker's stand, a loose line of rifle-armed men stood guard.

Wentworth circled the mob and approached one of the guards. Before he could get within speaking distance, the man's rifle leaped to his shoulder and he fired almost point-blank. A quick fall, a roll beneath the feet of fighting men alone saved Wentworth. He was up in an instant and darting back to where Nita crouched.

"They won't let me through," Wentworth said swiftly. "I guessed wrong on this mob. They're not going to kill the Senators. They're intended to keep anyone from reaching them and giving warning. We've got to get through."

Even as he spoke, three of the riflemen slipped around the crowd and came deliberately toward where they hid. Wentworth glanced at his watch. Five minutes before the attack on the Senators had been promised. There wasn't time to retreat and dodge these men in the shadows. In some way, he must force his way through this fighting crowd and reach the shaft, get below to the Senators. Once there, his quicker trained perceptions might foil the attack. Everything depended on that.

Wentworth's hands were knotted until they ached. He stared at the three men coming toward him. He could not use his two guns against them. Probably they were innocent of any wrong intent simply following orders. Yet, short of shooting them, how could he enter? It would take a half hour to circle to that precipice over the shaft and get down.

Even if he himself could manage, that would not be sufficient for he must have someone to drop him down to the Senators' level in the cage. That must be operated from above. He must drive his way through that mob, past those armed guards; he must take Nita with him to operate the cage, and he must do it in five minutes or the eleven Senators, feasting below upon a block of silver, would be doomed, and with them would fall the independence of the nation! The United States would be merely a private corporation in the hands of an unscrupulous gang of killers and thieves!

Five minutes....

THOSE THREE riflemen cautiously advanced to within a dozen yards of where Wentworth and Nita crouched in the shrubbery. Wentworth flung a desperate glance about. Five minutes between the Country and doom, five minutes to penetrate the mob, descend the shaft… Abruptly the Spider laughed, a soft but a wild sound.

"Come, Nita," he whispered and raced silently toward the steam-shovel. He threw himself to the firing platform behind the vertical boiler, glanced at the steam-gauge, barely smothered a shout of triumph. The pressure was high!

"Into the coal bin, quickly," he whispered to Nita. "You'll be out of reach of bullets there."

He whirled to the levers that operated the giant machine. The steam-shovel was a huge, awkward thing thirty feet long with a shed roof that cast a black shadow upon the platform. At its forward end a giant scoop armed with digging claws was attached to a steel beam that could thrust it forward like a battering ram to scoop up earth, swing it to either side, or lift it high into the air.

On each side beneath the truck were huge caterpillar-treads which, operated from the same engine that manipulated the shovel, could move it clumsily forward or back.

The riflemen advanced another five yards, their guns grasped alertly before them in both hands. Wentworth, invisible in the shadows beneath the shed roof, tightened his lips into a thin smile. It was not an unbeatable plan. The machine would move slowly, heavily. But he counted greatly on surprise. With a wrench he threw the giant caterpillar treads into gear. At the same moment he snatched at the lever that operated the shovel. With a hiss, an explosive belching of steam, the machine swung into operation like a dragon out of hell.

The claw-armed shovel swung viciously at the riflemen as

they flung guns to their shoulders. If it struck them... They did not wait for that. They scattered with a wild discharge of bullets that whined futilely toward the sky. A groan, a clanking clatter of steel, and the huge machine crawled forward, straight at the crowd. Wentworth kept the claw-shovel moving. He swung it from side to side, close against the ground, like a mighty flail. He wrenched it in close against the end of the machine's truck, then jabbed it forward like a battering ram.

Men in the crowd were screaming now. Rifles spurted powder flame from a score of points. Wentworth crouched low behind a spotty shield of levers and gears, continued to operate the shovel, using his hands on the foot pedals. A bullet glanced off a steel upright and screamed through the darkness. Men scattered from his lumbering path.

A side-swing of the shovel smashed the wagon from which Sinclair had been speaking, hurled the fragments flying like shrapnel after fleeing men. Above the mechanical clatter and shoutings of the crowd, Wentworth caught a roar of anger behind him. He jerked about in time to see a man fighting to mount the shovel's step. Even as he watched, a hunk of coal whistled through the air and bounced off the arm by which the man still clung. The hand flinched loose and the man tumbled to the ground. Nita was a perfect rear guard, fighting—with bullets of coal!

The crowd had scattered completely now, staring with incredulous, puzzled eyes at the lurching mechanical behemoth which clanked through their midst. Shadows were dense on the platform. They could glimpse a man who lay there but his presence meant little to them. A few tried tentatively to advance. But the slashing scoop, a scattering of pistol bullets over their heads, discouraged them.

Ahead loomed the last obstacle, a cordon of riflemen thrown about the shaft. They bunched together loosely and pumped bullets. Lead whanged into the boiler, pinged on levers all about Wentworth. A man in the crowd screamed with a wound and Tony Sinclair bellowed defiance.

"You're killing men!" he shouted. "Up and at the guards, comrades!"

Was it possible that Tony Sinclair guessed the purpose of this advance and fought with him? Wentworth did not know, but the men failed to rally. It made the guards' fire more cautious. Wentworth halted the lurching side-swing of the shovel, drew it in close against the machine's nose. It served as an additional shield. He was almost upon the riflemen now. Abruptly, he kicked a lever with his palm and the scoop darted forward with its steel-taloned claw. The riflemen scattered, the steam-shovel clanked on and Wentworth seized the guiding-wheel again, flung the truck broadside in front of the shaft.

HE JERKED open the furnace door and tossed in a dozen bullets from the gun belt he had taken from Rob. Then he caught Nita by the hand and raced with her to the engine that operated the elevator cage in the shaft.

"There are white stripes on the iron cable of the shaft," Wentworth barked at her. "They mark the depth of levels. Count thirteen of them, then slam on the brakes... like this!" He showed her how to operate the eccentric engine. He had to move swiftly for already the crowd had overcome its terror at the charge of the mechanical monster. They were rushing toward him. Wentworth sprang toward the shaft. Behind him a scattered fusillade broke out—the bullets he had tossed into the boiler fire had been ignited by the heat. They would harm no one, but the crowd took fright again, darted frantically for cover.

"Lower away!" he shouted.

Because Nita was inexperienced in the operation of the cage, she stopped it about five feet above the level of the thirteenth drive where the Senators were being banqueted. Wentworth crouched, leaped to the lip of the tunnel—and cursed, snatching for his gun!

Three men were crouched there, three men with pistols in their hands. Rage twisted Wentworth's face. These were Sinclair's underlings. They must be in on the plot to kill the Senators for they made no attempt to fire. They rushed with clubbed guns. Obviously they wanted to make no sound that might alarm the Senators and draw them from the maw of the trap that Sinclair had set.

Wentworth was desperate as the three closed warily in upon him. Not more than two minutes could remain before the blow that would wreck the country was struck here in the depths of the earth.

Two minutes....

As the three rushed in, Wentworth flung himself flat on the floor at the brink. Two of the guards were too close to catch themselves and stumbled over his prone body, pitched with smothering cries into the shaft. Their screams were cut off by an

Sinclair, in overwhelming terror, plunged past him—the last man to go.

Wentworth hurled his vial of explosive into the mouth of the tunnel.

echoing splash. Instantly Wentworth was up, wrestling with the third man. He knew what the splash meant. There was a sump at the foot of the shaft, a pit into which the drainage of the mine seeped to be pumped to the surface. Those two men would be kept busy for a while….

The third guard slashed viciously with his revolver. A smashing right to the chin drove him back. A left sent him reeling to the lip of the shaft. He wavered, throwing his arms wildly, pitched downward into the sump with his fellows. Without a second's pause, Wentworth whirled and ran along the tunnel. Back along this level somewhere the Senators revelled at a banquet, back along this level death would strike suddenly and terribly. What form would it take? What could he, one man, do against the hordes of the syndicate?

His feet pounded along the brilliantly illuminated passageway. The walls here, too, had been decked with bunting and ahead of him now Wentworth could hear the quick, maddening rhythm of a rumba. Hell, dancing, too! That meant women— dancing girls. Sinclair was doing a thorough job of entertaining.

A bend in the tunnel and Wentworth halted, staring with incredulous eyes. He was abruptly aware that the intense heat of the mine had given way to refreshing coolness. He saw the reason. Dry ice had been stacked around the walls of the chamber where the banquet was spread and constantly whirring batteries of electric fans kept the air circulating.

CHAPTER 9
THE DEATH-TRAP

I N THE middle of the large chamber, lit luridly by the flare of a hundred torches thrust into sockets in the walls, sat a huge block of silver that glittered with a dazzling sheen. It was pure metal and men must have worked for hours over it to polish the oxidization of centuries from its surface and leave the silver shining clear. There was no cloth upon it, but doilies of priceless linen.

Wine bottles were everywhere. Two spilled their red blood upon the silver of the table. Men in evening dress, were lolling in gilded chairs. From the shadows the rumba orchestra played. And a dancing girl spun and whirled upon the silver table. She was entirely nude except for two overlarge fans of ostrich plumes which she flicked with suggestive half-revelations of her exquisite shape. Her hair glistened like silver, her eyes shone.

The music halted abruptly and the girl sprang down from the table. A stout Senator whom Wentworth recognized reeled to his feet and staggered after her into the shadows while his companions guffawed. A deep voice boomed out and Wentworth wrenched his attention to the head of the table.

That voice couldn't be... but it was! Roscoe Sinclair stood at the head of the table. His white hair never was more sleekly combed, his massive face never more jovial. But why was he here where death would strike? A girl clad in a sheath of green, a silken gown that modeled every line of her figure, caught his hand and sprang to the table. Wentworth saw then that the apparent modesty of her long sleeves and high neck were a sham. The dress was as translucent as glass. The pink loveliness of her body shone through sheer silk. She struck an attitude. A man reeled to his feet and snatched at her, but she evaded him with a subtle swaying of her hips, began to sing in a provocative, baby voice....

Wentworth's mind was not upon the bacchanalia in progress but upon Sinclair's presence. What could that mean? The man certainly would not remain in this chamber if death were to strike. Yet he himself had set the hour, had taunted Wentworth with the fact that he would be helpless to assist the men upon whom the nation's very life depended.

It would do no good to cry a warning to these men, do no good to take Sinclair at gun-point. The Silver King would merely sneer at him, would refuse to reveal the potential death weapon. But what could the trap be?

Without warning, the blow fell. A rolling concussion beat upon the room, made the flames of the torches leap, stopped the music in discordant mid-beat. The Senators started to their feet. The girl froze with arms enticingly offering herself, but that was automatic. Her face was haggard with fear.

Wentworth sprang into the room.

"Flee for your lives!" he shouted. "The cage is waiting. Run! Run! This is another attempt to murder you!"

Wentworth caught a glimpse of Sinclair's amazed face. Then the Silver King turned his back on the fleeing men, the screaming women and stared up the dark low passage from which the roar of the explosion had come and which now echoed to another room, the tumultuous thunder of—Good God?—*water!*

In a flash, Wentworth understood, that blast had not been intended to collapse the shaft, to close the level in which the senators fled. It had released that underground river of long ago which only recently had been dammed.

That river had a temperature of one hundred and seventy degrees! If any of these men escaped death by drowning, he would be scalded to death even as he struggled upward through the shaft!

Wentworth's hand flew to the kit he carried always beneath his arm. There was a chance, a slim chance. Sinclair whirled to stare at him. Behind him, Wentworth spotted glimmering lights up that black tunnel of steaming waters. Lights that flickered redly. What in heaven's name could that be?

Wentworth's fingers were flying as he stared into the tunnel. He held two small vials of liquid. They held two component parts of trinitrototuolene, harmless each to itself, but combined forming one of the most powerful explosives known to man, a device invented by his friend Professor Brownlee. The flicker of lights rushed nearer—and the Spider saw and understood. THE KILLERS were making triply sure of their kill. Upon the surface of that boiling flood of super-heated water, burning oil bubbled and foamed. An avalanche of boiling water, surfaced with liquid flame! And the Spider, one lone man, stood in its path, stood between that devastating cataclysm and the destruction of the nation!

Sinclair shrieked in sudden, overwhelming terror and plunged past Wentworth, the last man to go. Wentworth hurled his vial of explosive into the mouth of the level that murderers had made the channel of a river of flame!

He spun and flung himself flat on the floor in the protection of a sharp angle of the tunnel. Behind him, hell burst loose. A blast of air swept over him. A hollow roar battered his ear drums, seemed to crush his skull. He drove himself to his feet, flashed a light back into the room of revelry and death.

The flatness had been blown out by the blast. The roof of the drive had been dropped to act as a dam in the path of the flood. It blocked the tunnel completely, but even as Wentworth stared at it, trickles of water, from which steam arose, began to force through.

Far ahead, as he ran, he could see Sinclair's heavy body racing. He saw the man reach the end of the level, clamber into the cage. Instantly the cage whipped upward. For a moment, Wentworth stared incredulously. Then a shout of rage tore from his throat. Sinclair had left him to die in this trap of death!

Without a second's pause, Wentworth flung himself at the ladder that ran the full depth of the shaft. With frantic hands he clawed his way upward. There was no way of telling how long that petty dam of collapsed rock would hold the furious waters. Not long, certainly. He figured his chances rapidly. He knew there were at least three levels below the one on which the banquet had been staged. When the river broke through, it would pour into the sump, flood those three levels and push upward. Probably it would rise all the way to the mouth of the shaft and overflow because of the enormous pressure behind it, but its rise would be slower and slower.

It would have to flood each level it reached. Fissures would drain part of it. Still, he had a half-mile to climb and the river made a terrific flood. A wild laugh gusted from Wentworth's lips. The Spider had a chance.

A sweep of air rushed upward past him, air from the gates of hell. It seemed to bake his skin as it roared past. He drove his weary arms and legs to more frantic efforts. The dam had burst. The flood of angry waters was loose. He heard it gush from the level mouth, a second Niagara bellowing as it poured into the sump. How long did he have now to reach the top? That rush of waters was enormous.

Wentworth strained his neck backward to peer toward the mouth of the shaft. Dimly, like, a pin-prick in the skies, he saw the gleam of lights high above him. The mouth of the shaft. It was an immeasurable distance. Sternly he drove himself. Steaming vapors rose about him, draining his strength. The bubbling heat of the waters, swelling with the pressure from beneath, made gurgling sounds that reverberated up the shaft. Level after level filled rapidly. The boiling flood seemed racing joyfully to seize its prey.

His arms and legs moved woodenly, almost without feeling. His heart-breaking labors lifted him slowly—slowly. And now Wentworth knew the waters were gaining! They would continue to gain, they would overtake him in the end despite all he could do!

ABRUPTLY A new sound broke into the monotonous lethal purring of the water—metallic, mechanical sounds. Wentworth stared aloft, saw movement at the top of the shaft. He shouted wildly. The cage was coming down! He squeezed his body against the ladder. The water filled the last level below him with a throaty gulp, pushed on more rapidly after its escaping prey. It was scarcely ten feet below him and had only the shaft to fill. Even while the cage dropped to his assistance, he must struggle upward. The elevator swished past him and smacked the water thunderously. Steaming liquid splashed up the sides of the shaft, actually licked Wentworth's feet. He jerked them to safety just in time, fastened his fingers like talons into the latticed side of the cage and clambered to its top, grasped the steel cable on which it hung, leaving the awkward ladder.

Up and up the waters crawled while he clung to the rope above the cage, feet braced on the twin iron supports that held the elevator. Lights had long since been extinguished when the water short-circuited the mine. He dragged out his pocket-torch, flung its beam downward. Six inches below his feet, the steaming water gurgled. In the instant he watched, it climbed an inch.

Frantically he flung the light about him. As he stood, his head was just above the floor of a working tunnel. If he could get his entire body above that point, he would gain minutes, precious minutes of life. When the water reached the mouth of the level, it would flow down into the underground chambers where ore had been mined. Instead of having to fill only the narrow shaft it would have to flood all that additional space before it could creep closer to him.

But to clear that level, to gain those precious minutes, he would have to raise his body four feet or more. He could do that by returning to the ladder which crawled up the opposite wall of the shaft. But if he did that, the elevator might be lifted suddenly and he would be left to die. There would be no second descent of the cage. Well, there was one other way—if his strained muscles could use it.

With flagging strength, he gripped the steel cable, twined his legs about it and began laboriously to climb upward. Even as he lifted his feet, the deadly waters closed over the braces on which they had rested. Death was that near! Inches, long, torturous inches at a time he struggled. His superb muscles had been drained beyond their strength by that frantic up-ladder climb, by the fighting turmoil of days past, by the long hours of rope shackles.

Wentworth battled to pull himself up another notch. His breath gasped out wildly. He strained, clenched his teeth—and sagged. He could not do it. To save his life, he could not force his muscles to drag him an inch higher. So close to safety and yet he was beaten. Gropingly he thrust out a foot, clinging with the last ounce, of his strength to the rope. He found a rung of the ladder, pushed out his other foot, and found another. He moved them up a round, and spanned his body horizontally across the gap between steel cable and ladder.

He waited, blood pounding in his ears, lungs pumping in gasps. His first warning would be the intolerable burning of his feet… What was that? Mad laughter sobbed with his gasps. He heard the first dry trickle of water into the level—and the boiling liquid had not touched him. His head sagged. He had won a momentary victory at least.

Suddenly a despairing cry ripped itself through Wentworth's throat, as if his soul were being torn from his body while he lived. His grip on the steel cable was slipping. It slid through his hands. His feet jerked off the ladder. He was falling—and the water was just below!

HE WAS being roasted on a griddle in Hell, Wentworth decided. There was someone else in Hell who knew him, evidently, for he heard his name called urgently, over and over. There was suffering in the voice. It was a woman. There were stirrings in his mind. Even the Devil had no right to make a woman suffer like that.

"Dick!" the voice cried. "Dick! Dick!"

It was Nita's voice. What, Nita in hell? Wentworth stirred on his griddle, pushed himself up from dark depths and opened his eyes. He looked upward into Nita's face. For long moments he looked at her and recognized those sweet blue eyes and was content with that. Then abruptly he remembered things.

He had been clinging to that steel cable, and his hands had slipped. He had plunged downward toward the super-heated waters. Abruptly he understood. His hands had slipped, but that had been because the cage had started upward. Instead of dropping into the water, he had fallen to the floor of the elevator as it was yanked clear of the flood. It must have been Nita who operated the cage.

"I'm all right, dear," he articulated slowly, and Nita sobbed with relief.

For an hour, Wentworth struggled against his fatigue. He was uninjured except for the bruises of his fall. His burns were slight, inflicted solely by such water as remained on the floor of the cage when it was yanked upward. He called on his superb strength, his marvelous recuperative powers and fought his way back to normality while Nita told him what had happened.

After she dropped Wentworth down the shaft in the cage when he first descended into the mine, she had fled back to the steam-shovel and secreted herself once more in the coal pile. The mob had failed to find her and almost immediately, it seemed, the Senators, the women and Roscoe Sinclair were reeled up in the cage. When Sinclair shouted that the underground river had broken loose, there had been a precipitate flight from the vicinity of the shaft.

As soon as they fled, Nita crawled from the coal and dropped the cage until she heard it strike the surface of the water. She then waited three minutes, to give Wentworth, if he had escaped, time to get aboard. She had lifted the cage slowly, checking every fifty feet for a minute so that if he had missed the cage at the bottom, he might get aboard higher up.

Wentworth lifted himself and stared down at the shaft, still lighted from above. An ugly flood was bubbling from the mouth, sending steaming water cascading down the mountain side. He and Nita circled the stream, pushed downgrade. Luckily the motorcycle had not been found in the panic rush to safety of the mine workers. They rode it slowly to the concrete strip, Nita, clinging behind Wentworth, then raced toward Denver, nearly fifty miles away.

Daylight was breaking over the mountains when Wentworth wearily tooled his motorcycle through the city's early morning traffic. Finally he halted beside a parked taxi.

"Dearest," Wentworth told Nita. "Go to your hotel and

phone Ram Singh." He smiled wearily. "Yesterday was Labor Day."

Nita dismounted and faced him anxiously, her blue eyes worried. The taxi chauffeur peered out at them with a grin. Nita had scrubbed most of the coal dirt from her face and arms, but much of it had clung to her clothing. Wentworth smiled at her.

"I'm going to get some sleep, beautiful," he reassured her. "An hour or two. You'd better do the same. Then I'll call you at your hotel and find out what you've learned from Ram Singh."

"You swear to that?" Nita asked softly, gazing directly into Wentworth's weary, blue-gray eyes.

For answer, he kissed her. Then he pushed her toward the taxi, jazzed the motorcycle engine, and spurted forward.

"Hurry, dear," he called back. "That phone call is important."

He leaned the motorcycle around a curve, wrenched the throttle wide and vanished in a swirl of blue exhaust-smoke. Nita sprang to the taxi. She started to order pursuit, then hesitated, biting her lips. That phone call was important, and if Dick didn't want her to follow him, she stood small chance of doing it successfully.

CHAPTER 10
THE SPIDER DIES

BUT NITA knew her lover. If he left her, it was because danger threatened—peril that he preferred to face alone. "The Tabor house," she told the driver slowly.

At the Tabor, Nita went haughtily through the ornate lobby

while attendants gaped. Once in her room, she called Washington. While she waited for the call, she bathed hurriedly and dressed in fresh white linens, a chic suit with puffed shoulders, garnished with red, a hat that chimed with it. The phone rang and she darted to it. Ram Singh's sharp accents were excited.

"The House has passed the bill," he told her rapidly. "The Senate will vote as soon as Senator Calloway gets here. He's flying from Chicago. When he arrives, the bill will go through. Tell the *sahib* that the session is to be held open until Senator Calloway gets here."

Nita's words were as staccato as his own. "Try to delay Senator Calloway," she said. "He is an honest man, but in this case misguided. There must be no violence, but, Ram Singh, everything depends on you!"

"Han, Mensahib!" the Hindu agreed.

Nita spun from the phone, hands clenched at her sides. Two hours, Wentworth had said. In two hours he would call. But minutes were precious. Even if the Senators left Denver for Washington, at once, there would not be any too much time. If Calloway got there first… She called a newspaper to find when the party was leaving. The editor understood the Senators were remaining to investigate the Yellow Hornet disaster.…

She phoned Senator Reagh's hotel and got through to the wiry little southerner, spilled out her information.

"I know," he said quietly. "I am flying east at once so my companions can look into this matter. My vote will tie Calloway's and block action until my colleagues arrive. I…" He

The guards sprang toward the mouth of the shaft. A man's masked face

thrust into view—and two hands filled with flame-spitting guns.

choked off with a gasp. Over the wire came a sound like feet beating on an attic floor.

Nita signaled the operator frantically, finally got the senator's hotel. "Quickly!" she gasped. "Senator Reagh is being attacked in his room!"

She flung from the phone and raced a taxi to Senator Reagh's hotel She found the place in a turmoil. Reagh had been strangled with a garrote. Police were taking charge. They glared suspiciously at the spruce young woman in white. Nita hurried from the building. She must find Wentworth. She *must!*

A taxi spurted from the rank and rolled up to where she stood forlornly on the curb. Frowning, she entered, glanced at the driver. It was the same man who had driven her a brief while before to the Tabor. His eyes were large with surprise as he recognized her. That rugged woman in breeches had become a lovely girl… An inspiration struck Nita abruptly.

"Where is Mr. Sinclair's home when he's in Denver?" she questioned rapidly.

The driver told her. It was four blocks from where Wentworth had left her!

"Take me there," she snapped at the driver, "and do it fast."

The taxi raced up Capitol Hill, through tree-shaded streets, curved up a drive to a resplendent mansion. Nita paid the driver off, told him to wait and walked calmly up the steps. The door was ajar, and hand on the bell button, she hesitated.

Then she pushed her way in abruptly, unannounced. Loud voices rumbled through the halls. They came from behind closed doors to her right.

"You killed him, Spider," a man grated venomously, "and we don't need the police to settle this little affair. You'll get yours right now." A harsh laugh interrupted the words. "We'll just say you tried to escape."

NITA CROUCHED against the door, all her fears confirmed. Weary as he was, Dick had thrust into new danger. Obviously someone in this room held her Dick at gun-point. They were accusing him of murder, knew his identity. Suddenly she heard Wentworth's brittle voice.

"Sorry to contradict you, gentlemen," he said in the gay mocking tones she knew so well. "But if you were to attempt to pull the trigger, a machine-gun would begin working on you from behind. Ah, you don't believe it? Charlie," his voice was raised now. "Charlie, open the door, but don't stand in line of any bullets. Just push the door open and stand ready with the machine-gun."

Nita gasped. How did Dick know she was there? Had he glimpsed her through a window? She smiled. It did not matter how he knew. She stepped behind the wall, twisted the knob and pushed the door violently. She made her voice deep.

"Okay, boss," she croaked hoarsely. "I got de chopper ready."

Curses within, a woman's scream, a single shot ripping the air to shreds, then Wentworth calling calmly....

"All right, Charlie, just hold them that way," he said. There was a slight jerking break in his voice as if he were moving swiftly. "Elsa, stand still, Charlie is no respecter of ladies. Black, Tony, get back! Charlie...."

"You can't get away with this, Spider," boomed the voice of Tony Sinclair.

"Sorry to contradict you," said Wentworth suavely. "Black, tie up Tony and do a good job of it. I'm going to test the knots. Bessie, tie up Elsa. Be quick, or this gun might put a neat hole in your fair white arm."

Nita sighed with relief. Dick had a gun now. Everything was all right. But she did not show herself. She waited. She knew from what Wentworth said that Bessie Kendall, Harry Black and Elsa were all in the room. But who had been killed and who had threatened Wentworth? Those things would have to wait.

"Okay, Charlie," Wentworth called again. "I've got the situation well in hand. Bring the car to the side entrance. Then cover the back of the house."

Nita slipped out again. She drove one of Sinclair's high-powered sedans from the big garage to the side entrance. She knew that her last instructions, "to cover the back of the house," were without meaning. It was a subtle way of telling her to get clear. She scribbled a note, advising Wentworth of the situation in Washington and fastened it to the steering wheel of the sedan, then had her taxi take her to the Tabor. In a second cab, she sped back to the Sinclair home.

The sedan she had parked at the side entrance was gone. Police were all over the place. They admitted her and Elsa ran into her arms with a little whimpering cry.

"Daddy was murdered!" she sobbed. "The Spider stole his body! He strangled another man, too—Daddy's bodyguard—and took his body also."

Nita stood rigid, her arms about the girl. "Daddy?" she asked. "You mean Roscoe Sinclair?"

"Yes," Elsa gasped out. "He was—strangled! Just like all those other men, and…."

A gray-haired police officer in civilian clothes glowered at them.

"We'll get the Spider," he snapped. "We know what his car's like and the radio patrol is after him. He's the one that's been killing these Senators in Washington and everywhere else." His lips grinned in a grimace that was not mirth. "The Spider," he jeered, "is just a murdering rat strangling men from behind."

Words rushed to Nita's lips but she choked them down. This man might be trying to goad her into speech. But how could Dick get to the Senators, speed them eastward to defeat the villainous measures of the Silver Syndicate if he was "fleeing from the police radio patrols? Police and the filers of the syndicate were closing in upon him. And the hours were speeding by, the hours that meant defeat, while the Spider could only flee.

A telephone bell jangled and the gray officer strode to it "Inspector Burnside speaking," he growled. He listened and a slow joyous smile spread across his mouth. "That's swell!" he reared into the phone. Burnside looked the women over slowly, toying with his moment, enjoying himself.

"What… what's swell?" It was Elisa who spoke, breathless. Burnside grinned at her benignly. He said, "It *is* swell. The Spider is dead!"

EACH WORD was a knife—stabbing Nita to the heart. She

closed her eyes and felt darkness swirling upon her, felt horror and despair and all hell swirling about her.

"No, no!" The words might have been a scream, but Nita locked them in her own breast. If Dick had fallen! He had not—he could not fall!

Fiercely she cried that within her, but she knew it was only her hope that spoke. She opened her eyes and realized that questions were flying back and forth around her. Tony Sinclair was smiling as widely as the inspector.

"That's swell, Inspector," he boomed. "That rat forced me to carry my own father's body out to the car." He sobered. "Did they get the body back?"

Inspector Burke nodded. "The Spider spilled over a precipice in the mountains. The car caught fire. There was very, little left of any of the bodies except your father's but we identified the Spider by his clothing and by a kit he carried under his left arm. It had in it certain articles that police know only the Spider carries, things he's been known to use on various occasions."

Nita's heart was pounding fiercely now. She and Dick had known that some day this must happen and she had sworn to carry on for him, to fulfill his vengeance, to wipe the slate clean of his enemies. She must be brave. She drove grief from her mind, looked about her.

"There's something funny, though," said Burnside. "Did you know your father wore a wig?" He was regarding Elsa with somber eyes.

The girl shook her head. "He didn't," she said flatly. "It's a favorite—a favorite game of ours for me to rumple his hair

152

and pull it. He didn't wear a wig. It was somebody disguised as father!"

The people standing in the hall stared at each other. What could that strange discovery mean? Tony Sinclair was frowning. The girl was not looking at Harry Black, but at Tony. She crossed to him slowly. "What does it mean, Tony?"

Nita's own mind was swift to the problem. If someone had been posing as Sinclair and had been killed, then all these appearances of Sinclair at the scenes of crimes might be faked. She shook her head abruptly. If there had been a false Sinclair working with the Assassins and then the genuine Sinclair had been killed, that would make sense, but this mix-up....

She pressed a hand wearily to her forehead. Dick would have to solve that problem, it was too much for her. A wrench of pain twisted her red lips bitterly. Dick would never solve another problem for her. She would have to work alone now. Oh, *Dick, Dick*....

The dooming words rang in Nita's ears as she sped downtown to the hotel of the Senators. *The Spider is dead.* Dear God, they had another meaning for her. *The world has come to an end.* She bowed her head, strangling a sob that sprang unbidden into her throat. She jammed her fists against her red mouth, the red mouth that Dick had kissed. Sobs choked her. They battered against her will, racked her. Her shoulders wrenched.

The taxi halted before the hotel and the driver swung the door open. White-faced, dry-eyed, Nita stepped from the cab. She was like a woman of marble. The door opened to her knock. A strange man beckoned her in.

SHE STEPPED inside. The door clapped shut and the man pointed a pistol at her. Nita did not flinch. As if bullets could hurt more than the pain already within her breast. "What is the meaning of this?" she asked coldly. She glanced about, saw the ten Senators who remained alive were sitting awkwardly about the room covered by two other men with guns.

"The meaning, girl friend," the man with the grin said, "is that you're the dame phoned Reagh a while ago. Lucky I was listening in and heard you or there might have been trouble."

"I'm afraid I don't understand."

"You're just in time for the party, girl friend," the man continued mockingly. He turned toward the Senators. "All right, stuffed shirts," he jeered, "get going. Or does somebody want a touch of the cord here and now?"

He pulled a silk-woven cord from his pocket. Nita recognized it as a garrote such as had been used to kill other Senators. The legislators did not hesitate. One and all they stood, staring dumbly, like sheep in a slaughter house. They filed slowly out, descended to autos where more men with hidden guns took them in charge. Nita went with them woodenly. There was nothing else she could do.

An hour later they alighted by a mine shaft half-hidden by scrubby undergrowth. A few slatternly buildings were rotting in disuse and wind-twisted trees looked like the skeletons of mortals who had been broken on the rack.

"This," said the man of the black eyebrows, still grinning, "is the mine you're going to inspect. Who wants to see it first?"

The Senators still stood meek as sheep. The man singled out one. "How about you?"

"I don't know what you mean," stammered the Senator. He was stout and had sparse white hair. Bags sagged beneath his eyes.

"This," said the gunman. He caught the Senator by the arm, thrust him violently toward the shaft, paused at the brink while the Senator fought weakly against his hold. "The shaft is a mile deep," said the gunman. "Go ahead and look at it!"

He pushed. With a hoarse despairing shout, the Senator pitched into the black opening. His voice shrieked, cut off suddenly. His murderer smiled at the nine Senators and at Nita.

"See?" he asked almost gently.""It doesn't take long. Who's next?" His eyes fell on Nita. "Nope, not you," he said and his eyes glistened. He touched his lips with his tongue. "I'm going to save you till last, baby," he said. "You're too good looking to die a...."

"Freeze!" a voice cut harshly in upon his words. "Freeze and reach for the sky." The voice seemed to issue from the mouth of the shaft!

The gunman gasped, whirled with his gun ready. A pistol spoke sharply, but it wasn't his. The man gasped again. He bent gently over at the waist, dropped to his knees and plunged forward dead. The five other guards sprang toward the mouth of the shaft. A man's masked face thrust into view there—a man with two hands filled with flame-spitting guns. Two more gunmen sprawled.

Nita laughed aloud, happiness singing in her heart. In all the world, only one man could thus thwart the assassins, only one man—the Spider.

"DICK! DICK!" The words rose unbidden to her lips, but she stopped them there. She had known all the time that he could not be killed. She had known it. Sudden fear stabbed through her. Of course, Dick could be killed. He was battling three men now, exposed to their gunfire.

She flung herself toward the body of the closest fallen gunman, snatched up his gun and fired it twice straight at the criminal nearest her. The man turned a surprised face, stood motionless, staring at her. His eyes closed then and he collapsed. The other two assassins whirled to meet this new attack and the guns of the masked man spoke twice more.

The gun dropped from Nita's hand. She started to fling herself toward the shaft, toward Dick, who had been dead and now was resurrected. She stumbled forward two paces, then halted, her arms hanging, limply, tears crowding to her eyes. Her kiss would be the caress of Judas!

So Nita stood with only her eyes to speak her love while the Spider climbed out of the shaft, peered back down into that dark deathly mouth.

"Think you can make it, West?" he called. He turned to the other Senators. "I had a net fastened across the shaft a little way down, just in case I couldn't get into action fast enough. I was lucky enough to learn their plans in advance."

He turned to Nita, swept her a faultless bow. "Pardon me if I don't remove my hat. I should like to in tribute to a brave and very lovely lady. Your shots were very timely."

The thin-haired, pink head of Senator West showed above the mouth of the shaft. When he stood erect his face was crimson with anger.

"Some one shall pay for this," he asserted. It was the beginning of declamation.

"No one will pay unless we get back to Washington fast" Wentworth snapped. "They're putting up the Silver Bill for passage this afternoon. There's a plane down in the valley. We'll have to get there fast. The Silver bunch is back of all this."

"Who are you?" West asked suddenly. Wentworth grinned at him, firm lips curving beneath the black mask that concealed his eyes. He touched a cigarette-lighter lightly to the forehead of the nearest dead gunman, and a spot like blood gleamed as he crossed to the next corpse, a spot that was the sinister seal of the Spider!

Senator West gasped, fell back a pace and almost toppled again into the shaft. One of his colleagues stepped hurriedly forward and caught his arm. For a moment as he stooped to brand the other dead, Wentworth continued to smile, then he grew grave and began to snap out orders.

"Down the hill fast," he barked. "And remember! You've got to block that bill or maybe the Spider will pay *you* a call."

As the men straggled hurriedly down the hill, Wentworth called to Nita. "Brave Lady, I shall do myself the honor of escorting you personally. Would you mind waiting just a moment?"

"Oh Dick, *Dick,*" she breathed. "I thought you were dead! And yet I knew they couldn't… couldn't…."

Wentworth patted her hands. "Swell work, beautiful," he

whispered. "Quick thinking, too, not running to me. But I knew I could depend on you. I always can."

They rounded a clump of trees and the open valley spread below them. The first of the Senators was climbing aboard a giant Boeing transport, assisted deferentially by a masked man Nita recognized as Ram Singh.

"We don't stand a chance of reaching Washington in time to block it," Wentworth said. "The Senators will vote within two hours. It will take us at least seven to get there." He shook his head. They were walking slowly now, keeping distance while Ram Singh herded the Senators aboard. "The leader of the Assassins—I still don't know who he is—is still alive," Wentworth continued. "All I've won are a few minor victories, and the showdown finds me hundreds of miles from the scene."

"But Dick!" Nita clung to him. "You can't mean we're beaten!"

Wentworth disengaged her hands with a little warning tap, squeezed her arm as he helped her into the plane. "That's in the spinning of the Fates," he said quietly, then smiled in self-mockery. "Or perhaps, in the web of the Spider!"

CHAPTER 11
BLACKMAIL IN THE AIR

THE ROAR of mighty engines drowned any reply Nita might have made and the giant transport-plane trundled across the field, slid lightly into the air and rose in a slow climbing curve eastward. Washington lay seven hours of break-neck flying in that direction.

Wentworth turned to the forward wall of the plane and fiddled with the dials of a radio. A loudspeaker overhead began to pour out strains of jazz. Wentworth eyed it speculatively, glanced at his watch.

"I've got a half hour, darling," he said. "Then I've got to start things moving." He looked up. Senator West had rolled forward and stood confronting him.

"See here, fellow…" Senator West began portentously.

"Oh, Jack," Wentworth called. The cockpit door slapped open and a man masked like Wentworth popped out. It was Ram Singh, but to prevent identification, his turban had been replaced by a uniform cap, his loose Hindu garb by a khaki uniform. His wiry body was alert.

Wentworth waved a hand toward Senator West and the others. "Keep them quiet. Herd this one back."

Nita was seated beside him now. Her hand reached out for his furtively so none could see. It must always be furtively—Their fingers intertwined, slim white fingers, brown strong fingers. Nita drew a deep slow breath.

"I—I thought you were dead, Dick."

Wentworth smiled without opening his eyes. He was weary, inexpressibly weary. And the greatest struggle was still to come. In half an hour, he must begin the final battle of this war….

Yet Wentworth, speeding eastward to that battle, sat relaxed, his lips smiling. He was a fighter gathering strength in his corner between the bells while seconds worked over him. Nita was his second. Her mere presence was a restorative that transcended any medical stimulants. He thrilled to the sweet apprehension of her voice when she said she had thought him dead.

"I made it seem I had died because the police were close behind me," he said slowly. "I had to be rid of them for a while to work out my plans. I knew that when I carried Sinclair's body and the gunman's from the place."

"Sinclair!" Nita exclaimed. "But it was only a man disguised as Sinclair!"

Wentworth shook his head. "No, Sinclair was murdered by the Assassins. He was innocent, simply profiting by the work of someone else. That someone—I don't yet know whom—posed as Sinclair in a disguise. I never could convince myself that a man in Sinclair's position would openly turn criminal. When I was taken prisoner after that fight in my plane, I detected that the man who condemned me was not Sinclair.

"That man was a trifle shorter and there was something not quite authentic about his voice. Also, he called me the Spider, but never Wentworth. Yet the real Sinclair knew my identity. I still did not grasp the situation in full. The final proof of Roscoe Sinclair's innocence was his presence with the Senators in the mine death-trap. I knew then that when he escaped, another attempt would be made to kill him. I tried to get to his Denver mansion in time to catch the killers in the act, knowing that then I would have a definite clue to the Assassins. I was too late. Sinclair had been murdered and hanged on a door to make it look like suicide." Wentworth paused.

"I was looking over the old man's papers for a clue when Elsa Willing walked in on me and screamed. Tony Sinclair rushed in with Bessie and Harry Black. They had all come to help Tony make peace with his father. A body guard of Roscoe Sinclair's came in and pulled a gun." He smiled at Nita.

"When I saw you in the taxi through the window—the others missed you because they were all facing me—I used the trick that you co-operated in so nicely, to distract the body guard. I partly strangled him, had to shoot down another guard who entered, from somewhere in the house after you left I took Sinclair's body, the gunman's, and also the unconscious guard away with me. Later I revived the guard and questioned him. He cracked and told about the plans for the murder of the Senators, but he apparently thought Roscoe Sinclair was the real leader. He attacked me when I relaxed a moment and I had to complete the job of strangling him.

"I disguised him as Sinclair, fixed up the other killer to look like me and sent Jackson out to wreck the car. He did a good job of it, I hear." Wentworth dug out a cigarette and he and Nita lighted up. "I raced out to the shaft then—I found out about that from the guard too—and managed to save the Senators. You know the rest."

"But if you had Sinclair's body and a gunman's," asked Nita, "why did you have to disguise a gunman like Sinclair? And what did you do with his body?"

Wentworth smiled thinly, glanced at his watch. "I have other uses for Sinclair's body," he said. "You'll find out about that later. It's about time to start the fireworks."

He strolled back to where Ram Singh lounged against a seat with the Luger in his hand.

"Okay, Jack," Wentworth said.

The Hindu looked at him inquiringly, answered by a slow nod. He turned and went forward swiftly. The eyes of the ten Senators were focused unswervingly on Wentworth's face.

"Gentlemen," he said. "Do you know who made these infamous attempts on your life? Do you know what was behind it? It was the Silver Syndicate, the organization that Sinclair headed."

Senator West reared to his feet. "Of course we know," he thundered and the ready blood began to crimson his face, even tinted the scalp beneath his scanty white hair pink. "That has been the reason for our investigations. We have learned a great deal."

"That's splendid," Wentworth said. "Then you will vote against the bill?"

"That sir," thundered West in his best forensic manner, "is an insulting question. Of course we will! It now has become our sole reason for living."

ABRUPTLY THE radio, which had been discoursing jazz, squealed, howled, and began to rasp words. "Calling the Senators' plane," it squawked, "calling the Senators' plane! I have a message for you. A picture was taken in the mine. A picture was taken in the mine just before the girl in green began to sing. Unless you vote as you have been told, that picture will be broadcast throughout the country. Senator West will be especially interested."

Wentworth whirled angrily toward the radio, reached it in two strides, switched it off. He spun toward the Senators.

"Blackmail!" he thundered. "They are threatening to show a

picture of you gentlemen drunk about Sinclair's banquet table. It would show that naked fan-dancer—show Senator West chasing her into the shadows. I'm afraid no one would think your intentions innocent, Senator West." He paused, went on angrily. "It's a damnable trick, but I'm sure you won't let it swerve you from your purpose, will you, gentlemen of the Senate?"

West dropped back in his seat "This is infamous," he gasped. "Infamous."

"You won't let it influence your vote, will you, Senator?" Wentworth insisted.

West looked flustered, finally heaved to his feet and cleared his throat.

"I hope no one can impugn the honesty of my intentions," he said heavily. "My record speaks for itself." He hesitated. "I love to serve my country, however, and I feel that if I permitted such a picture to be broadcast that my usefulness to my country would be at an end. I will have to vote for the Silver Bill!"

Wentworth goaded Senator West on his decision, pointed out the underhanded tactics of the Silver Ring, but West was adamant. He began an oration on the Silver Syndicate and its vile tactics, pointing out that there would be no question that it would carry out its threat about the picture. He had resisted bribery and threats, but now the menace was national ridicule and he could not stand it. Wentworth glanced at the other Senators. He saw that several were itching to get the floor and air their grievances. West in defense of his stand, was telling what the Silver Syndicate had attempted to do to him—how valiantly he had resisted bribery and threats.

Wentworth interrupted him. "I suggest, Senator West," he said, "that when you finish your speech you constitute yourself chairman in the absence of Senator Reagh. You gentlemen can then discuss your situation fully. Perhaps by the time we reach Washington, you will decide that you can vote for the measure."

He walked down the aisle, taking Nita with him, and drew across the plane a curtain that cut off the front part of the cabin from the rear. Then he rapidly buckled on a parachute pack and had Nita do the same. They forced open the door against the pressure of wind and slipstream and jumped into the twilight depths.

Two hours later, Nita was on a train traveling eastward. Wentworth was in a plane within one hundred and fifty miles of Washington, flying a special speed job that could crowd three hundred and fifty miles an hour.

Wentworth dropped his small, swift plane to Hoover field like a bullet, raced immediately to a taxi-rank and ordered a race to the Capitol. He leaned forward and switched on the radio the taxi carried for passengers. A lugubrious voice was speaking, the well known tones of Senator West.

"The Silver Syndicate offered me a fifty-thousand-dollar bribes and I refused them. They wanted only that I vote for their Silver Bill. Later, they told me that unless I did as they ordered I would be strangled to death as Racktat had been. I still refused. But this picture is insurmountable. We will be the laughing stock of the nation. We must yield."

ANOTHER MAN asked formally for the floor and got it. He went into details about the things they had learned about the Silver Assassins. He recited as absolute fact things at which Wentworth and Reagh had only guessed. "Even if it means our everlasting martyrdom," the man said vociferously, "we must vote against this bill."

Wentworth tapped on the glass that separated him from the driver.

"How long have these speeches been going on?" he asked.

"Damned near three hours," the taxi driver said excitedly. "Say, did you ever hear anything like it? These here Silver guys have been bribing and killing people to get their bills through. They're a bunch of crooks. Hell, I was for their bill before. But I'm agin it now."

Wentworth leaned back satisfied. If half the people reacted as the taxi driver had—if he could stop the bill, remove the leader of the Assassins... He stared out the window at dark trees sliding past. It was night and he caught the distant flare of widespread fires, houses ablaze. A rattle of rifles drifted down the night wind. A street was jammed with marchers and the taxi driver did a hurried right-about and fled to another avenue.

"All over town like that." He swore over his shoulder. "Them damned Silver Marchers have got the city by the ears. Damn' crooks!"

Wentworth's mouth was grim. Law enforcement was breaking down. If these silver measures passed, the nation would be helpless to resist the armed hordes of the Silver Assassins. He must triumph in the battle. Six blocks from the Capitol, Wentworth dropped from the taxi, crossed the street to where a long-nosed Lancia town car was parked. He entered the back. Instantly it was in motion.

Wentworth touched a button beneath the left side of the seat and the entire section of cushions slid forward, revolving as it moved. It contained a complete wardrobe of clothing. Wentworth's quick hands pulled out a tray with a brightly-lighted make-up mirror and he went to work swiftly on his face.

"How is it, professor?" he asked as he massaged in grease cream.

"I don't know exactly how it's going," Professor Brownlee's dry, abrupt words came back to the Spider as he worked. "I had the broadcasting apparatus rigged up in the plane, turned it into a studio as you asked, arranged for the re-broadcast at greater power and over the regular wavelengths. I rigged fully fifty receiving sets in the Capitol. If you don't think it was a job eluding those guards while I installed the radio gadgets, then you never tried burglary. That box you shipped east arrived hours ago and is ready."

"Have they voted?" Wentworth asked.

"They hadn't twenty minutes ago," Brownlee said. "Those speeches caused terrific repercussions. I think the syndicate has a dozen strong-arm men in the Senate cloakrooms. Lots of other men have been hunting the receiving sets, finding and destroying them, but there still are about a dozen squawking. The echoes in the dome conceal their exact location."

"That's fine," Wentworth said softly. His face had become wide and massive now. He reached into a drawer and drew out a sleek white wig, drew it on and inspected his reflection in the brilliantly-lighted glass. The face of Roscoe Sinclair peered back at him, but the eyes were blue-gray, not black.

WENTWORTH REACHED into another compartment and pulled out two small, curved bits of glass. There was a black spot on each that was just the size of Wentworth's iris. He rinsed these glasses with salt water and fitted them under his eyelids against the eye-balls. They were the new Zeiss invisible optical lenses, with false black irises painted on them. It was necessary to move the head instead of the eyeballs in looking from side to side, but they did change the color of the eyes. It was a trick he had learned from that notorious criminal who nearly triumphed over the Spider, the super-criminal who called himself the Fly.

Now the face was that of Roscoe Sinclair in every detail. Wentworth turned next to his clothing. "The radio trick worked like a charm in the plane," he said. "Ram Singh's voice threatening blackmail sounded exactly as if it were coming off the air. The Senators started making speeches immediately. Your hidden microphones turned the plane into a perfect broadcasting station."

Brownlee was frowning at the path of his headlights as he circled toward the Capitol. "I still don't understand all this," he said. "You've delayed the vote all right, but when your Senators do get here, they'll be afraid to vote against the bill because of this fake talk Ram Singh made about a photo that doesn't exist."

"The plane won't land here at all," Wentworth said coolly. "It's swinging in wide circles in the Middle west. You sent word to the Senate Chamber that Sinclair would be there personally?"

Brownlee nodded. "I did," he said, "and I understand that the senators decided that they would delay the vote until they had a chance to talk with Sinclair, though how you can produce a dead man, I don't see. Neither do I see why you don't want your Senators here."

"Just a minute, my good man," boomed Wentworth in the tones of Sinclair. "This has gone far enough. Will you be good enough to drive me to the Capitol?"

Brownlee's head jerked about. He jabbed the brakes and stared, his small eyes twinkling behind his glasses. His hand rose to stroke his silver-streaked goatee.

"Perfect!" he exclaimed. "Dick, you amaze even me sometimes."

Wentworth nodded curtly, still imitating Sinclair. "To the Capitol," he boomed.

He smiled grimly. It should be plain why he did not want the Senators here. Mere defeat of the Silver Bill would accomplish no permanent good. He was putting everything on one throw of the dice in an effort to achieve a final and devastating victory. If the dice went against him....

Wentworth's smile became twisted. But the dice of Fate must not roll wrong. He must win or the nation would crumble.

WENTWORTH SHOWED none of his anxiety, however. He went steadily to meet the four men who rushed toward him, peering at them beneath the simulated heavy brows of Roscoe Sinclair. Three of these were obviously strong-arm men. The fourth was a well-known Senator. The three guards formed a swift alert ring about him, watching the shadows. The Senator darted up.

"Thank God you've come," he said hurriedly. "It's terrible! Terrible!"

Wentworth blew out a puffing breath. So far the disguise had got by, but inside the lights would be stronger. He allowed a sardonic smile to twist his lips. He must play the part boldly. That was the point at which most disguises fell through. Men assumed the outward appearance of a certain identity and let their imitation end there.

When Wentworth assumed a false character, his very thinking changed. He spoke with the other man's voice. He moved with that man's peculiar stride, carried his head as the other did. Now he spoke with the gruff abruptness of Sinclair.

"I thought I had efficient men here," he cried angrily. "Do you call this efficiency?"

"I did my best to whip them into line," the Senator muttered. "When they refused to vote for the bill, I almost decided to get in touch with you although we have been given to understand not to mention your name even in connection with these affairs, much less call you. But the boys are jittery as hell. It's these radio broadcasts. It's like this in every state in the country, I understand. Just listen."

Raucous words were squawking from hidden radios. The echoes were confusing. It was impossible to tell the exact source of the sound. Wentworth allowed his face to become convulsed with anger.

The radios squawked and inwardly Wentworth applauded. If he had been there in the plane prompting the Senators they couldn't do a better job.

"Sinclair is a fiend," boomed West's bass. "He has blackmailed and bribed half the Senate. I stood firm against a fifty-thousand-dollar bribe. I stood firm against threats of death. But this, gentlemen, is beyond me. I was willing to die, but I am not willing to be branded a senile playboy. There must be some way we can defeat this ring and yet preserve our reputations. I feel that I am still of value to my country...."

Deferentially, the Senator opened the door of a cloakroom. Wentworth stalked through with the angry, belligerent stride of an outraged man. His quick eyes glanced about the room. Two men were standing in its center. They took one glance at him and bolted to the door. Wentworth identified their keen, sharp-lazy faces. He knew newspaper men when he saw them. Soon the extras would blazon forth that the Silver King was in the Capitol.

Wentworth strode to the table, put his back to it and stood with braced legs, hands locked behind his back, broad shoulders rolled forward and the heavy-jawed face of Roscoe Sinclair thrust out angrily.

"All right," he snapped. "Now, I'll have to straighten out the mess you've made. Get the Senators in here."

The Senator stared at him, loose lips gaping. What was the matter, Wentworth wondered. Had this hypocritical fool managed to penetrate his disguise? The lights were bright in here. They might well betray him if this man knew Sinclair well. But there could be no delay now. He would push this thing through. One cast of the dice... He took a choppy, forceful stride forward. "Hurry, fool!"

The instant the door closed behind him, Wentworth skipped to the door. He still must set the stage for the final act of his drama. Everything must go off with absolute smoothness, or....

He jerked the door open, peered down the corridor. Two men were just entering the hall with a long heavy box between them. One of the guards who had rushed to meet him was watching Wentworth with puzzled eyes.

"That box," Wentworth told him gruffly, pointing. "Have it brought in here."

With calm assurance that the men were used to obedience, Wentworth went back into the cloakroom and shut the door behind him. What was the meaning of the man's stare? Had he penetrated the disguise? Wentworth's hand slid beneath his coat, touched the two automatics that were strapped beneath his arms. He had small personal fears. He could always shoot his way clear against criminals. But the Spider never feared for himself. It was his country that was at stake. Should he call that man in and deal with him?

WATCHING, LISTENING, he saw the doorknob revolve, then turn back, but the door did not open. He took two swift steps toward it, then checked. The door was swinging inward. "Hurry," Wentworth barked in Sinclair's voice. "Don't take all day with that box."

The door opened and a man backed into the room. Wentworth saw that he was carrying the front of the box. He realized then the reason for that suspicious movement of the doorknob. The guard was solicitously assisting the men.

"On the table," Wentworth ordered, "then get out of here."

The three hurried out. Wentworth stood as before against the table, legs braced apart, belligerent head thrust forward. The door opened to admit two Senators. They nodded at him but he ignored them. They put their heads together and whispered. More men began to arrive by twos and threes until the cloakroom was packed! They watched the fake Sinclair covertly, but he ignored them all, staring straight ahead in angry silence.

Every time the door opened, he caught a fragmentary squawks from the radios "…that infamous scoundrel Sinclair…" He had reason to be angry in his assumed identity. But suppose some of these men knew Sinclair intimately. Suppose one of them penetrated his disguise. He must stand here and wait until they were in the room, must undergo their constant scrutiny. He felt his heart beating high in his throat, long slow throbs. He clenched his hands tightly, clasped them behind him. Presently the Senator who had first approached him pushed through the close-packed men, his loose lips grinning.

"All here, Mr. Sinclair," he said pompously.

"Gentlemen," Wentworth boomed in Sinclair's deep voice. He looked them all over slowly and said it again. "Gentlemen!"

There was something sardonic in the dooming word. Not a one of these men but who had yielded to bribery or threats to betray his country. The idea flicked through Wentworth's mind and sarcasm tinged his voice, made the Senators stir uneasily.

"Gentlemen of the Senate," Wentworth went on. "We have delayed too long in the battle. There is nothing left but retreat. It is my wish that you defeat the Silver Bill!"

A ripple of amazed voices spread over the room. Two or three uttered subdued shouts of applause. For the most part their faces looked stunned. Then as the purport of his statement penetrated, more and more joined in the low-toned applause. Wentworth flung out a hand in an abrupt gesture, glaring at them. Silence fell.

Wentworth knew that he must hurry, must finish his speech before the interruption of the Assassin's leader. His quick, searching eyes had failed to locate in the room any of the men whom he suspected of being the leader. But the killer's arrival might be announced by nothing more than a swift bullet!

"We have no choice but to defeat it," Wentworth went on. "Later we may return to the attack, but if we carry through now, all our operations will be exposed through sheer force of public opinion. I imagine—" his voice grew dry, "that you are no more anxious for that than I am. Defeat the bill. Let our defeat of that measure give the lie to these accusations that are being made!"

A man laughed aloud.

"Damned clever!" another shouted.

"That's the play, Sinclair!"

Wentworth stood unsmiling upon the chair. He had finished his speech, had won one move of the final battle, but only a minor point. Even when they defeated the Silver Bill, the fight was not won. There still remained the man who posed as Sinclair so cleverly.

He saw, too, that the Senators, and undoubtedly many others in both houses of Congress would be ready to obey when next this false Sinclair should speak. His own action in obtaining instant obedience of his order to defeat the Silver Bill was proof of that. No, the war was not over. Wentworth felt again the swift throb of prescience of danger. Yes, the leader and death were past due on the scene. He moved his hands in an abrupt gesture of dismissal and the Senators began to file out, the loose-lipped leader first of all.

As the man's hand reached for the knob, the door slammed inward, struck and hurled him to the floor. Four men charged in, four men who stalked past him without a sideways glance.

Three of the men wore the uniforms of police. The fourth was massive of body and his hair was a sleek mane of silver, it was the false Roscoe Sinclair—it was *the leader of the Assassins!*

The man shouldered his way roughly through the panicky Senators until he was half-way across the room, then halted with the three police at his back. He threw out his arms, index finger pointing stiffly at Wentworth in an accusing gesture.

"Arrest that man," roared the Assassins' leader. "He is an impostor. I am the real Roscoe Sinclair!"

CONSTERNATION FOUND voice among the Senators. They stared from one to other of these two Roscoe Sinclairs. Wentworth realized there was nothing to choose between. The Assassin's disguise was as perfect as his own, his mannerisms and his voice were as well studied an imitation of the Silver King's. "You lie!" he shouted in Sinclair's hoarse bellow. "You lie like a dog. You are the impostor. You dare not meet me face to face!"

The false Sinclair's bellow matched his own. "I dare not! Why—" His voice broke off in an inarticulate snarl. He pounded forward and men ducked and dodged from his furious path.

Wentworth waited his coming with head thrown forward.

He stepped down from his rostrum and glared. His keen gaze, narrowed behind the false black eyes, studied the disguise of the other man and bewilderment grew in his brain. Even his practiced scrutiny could detect no signs of make-up!

"You are the impostor!" he howled.

In the middle of his sentence, he sprang abruptly forward. His left hand snatched at the sleek silver hair, the nails of his right hand raked across the bulging jaws, then Wentworth sprang back to his chair. His right hand had found no make-up putty such as he had used on his own jaws, but his left held a silvery wig which he had snatched from the man's head. It revealed crisp black natural hair and showed also why he had found no makeup.

"See!" cried the Spider. "This man is the impostor! He wore a wig. Do you need further proof?"

Even while he shouted the words, Wentworth was watching the man he had unmasked. That man, the leader of the Assassins, the man who had killed scores and corrupted half the legislators of the nation for gold and profit, who had finally killed Roscoe Sinclair himself was—*was Tony Sinclair!*

"This man—" he shouted on, still flaunting the wig while his right hand crept toward his lapels, toward the butt of his automatic strapped beneath his left arm, "this man is the leader of the Assassins. He is Tony Sinclair! He and not Roscoe Sinclair bribed and threatened you Senators. He and not Roscoe Sinclair planned to profit from this career of crime. To that end, this man, Tony Sinclair, attempted to kill his own foster-father!

"He planned to marry his foster-father's ward and use the

vast resources he would thus inherit to overthrow our government. The mobs in the streets answer his commands. He is the criminal."

UNTIL THE moment when his finger-nails had raked across Tony's face and found no make-up putty there, Wentworth had not believed that Tony could be the chief Assassin. He had suspected Tony and Harry Black above all others, but used as he was to human beasts, he had not envisaged a man turning against his father. He had figured the motives in the cases of both Black and Sinclair and now he knew why the impersonation had been so perfect.

Tony had claimed to be the illegitimate son of Roscoe Sinclair. His features and build confirmed that. Even the voices and mannerisms were similar. A silvery wig, a few age lines on his face, had been the only disguise he needed.

Tony Sinclair had staggered back at Wentworth's denunciation, but he rallied while the amazed police stared from one to the other of the two men who accused each other, while the Senators stood stunned at the disclosures.

"I'm no criminal," Tony Sinclair boomed. "I came here in disguise, it is true, but only to confound this man. He, too, is an impostor."

Wentworth nodded, deliberately lifted his own wig from his head. "Yes, I am an impostor," he admitted. "My words have already revealed that fact. But I have brought Roscoe Sinclair himself here to accuse you, Tony. You did not kill him as you thought. I carried him away and revived him."

With a solemn nod Wentworth turned toward the table

where the long box rested. He stretched out a hand. This was his ace-in-the-hole, this was the play on which he had gambled everything to overcome the Assassins. But his hand reaching toward the box was rock-steady. He touched the lock of the box. The lid flew up. A man jerked his body erect within it like a released jack-in-the-box. The right arm of the man raised stiffly and pointed accusingly at Tony and—*the man was Roscoe Sinclair!*

"You, Tony, tried to kill me!" a deep voice boomed.

Tony Sinclair screamed. There was utter terror in his voice. He staggered back from that accusing finger as from a blow. Even as he reeled his hand flew to his coat lapel, slid within it. His lips had shrunk back from his teeth in a horrible grin. "Yes, damn you!" he screamed again. "And this time—"

He snatched his gun clear, but with the weapon leveled at his foster-father, he hesitated. He was staring at the man sitting in the box. The arm was still stiffly outstretched. The face was set and expressionless. The eyes staring, glazed.

"Tricked, by God!" Tony Sinclair snarled.

He jerked the gun's muzzle about toward where the Spider, quietly smiling at his victory, stood watching him. Even as the gun leveled, before Tony's furious fingers could contact upon the trigger, Wentworth's own automatic leaped from its holster and streaked flame straight at Tony's breast.

Tony wavered, swayed back on his heels, then forward again. His hateful eyes were fixed on Wentworth's face. A low curse tore from his throat. The Spider watched him warily, watched the hand that struggled against the numbness of approaching death, tried furiously to bring the gun to bear. Beads of sweat popped out on Tony's forehead. His lips moved soundlessly now. His gun hand swung straight down and the weapon clattered on the floor. The sound was terribly loud in the tense, silent room.

Abruptly the hate was wiped clear from Tony's face. His head swung about toward the man in the box. He took a single wooden step and pitched to the floor, his hands clawing at the table's edge. He writhed, rolled over on his back, and died. Wentworth smiled thinly down at the dead genius who had plotted a country's downfall and nearly achieved his ends. He looked up at old Roscoe Sinclair, still sitting rigidly with that accusing arm outthrust so that it pointed now toward the senators who had been the dupes of his foster-son. Wentworth turned to face the Senators.

"Roscoe Sinclair had no part in these crimes," Wentworth said heavily. "Every criminal act was contrived by his foster-son. The two hated each other, but Tony knew that the Syndicate could be counted on to take advantage of all the breaks that came its way. It would purchase the mines Tony wrecked, lobby for the bills he sponsored by bribery and blackmail. He overstepped himself when he tried to frame a young engineer out west, Harry Black, for his crimes, in order to have a scapegoat and to steal Black's fiancée.

"Tony had ideas about women, too. He planned to marry his foster-father's ward for Sinclair's money, then have Bessie Kendall, too."

WENTWORTH GLANCED toward the box and the still rigidly-pointing man. Professor Brownlee, Wentworth thought, had done an excellent job of fixing the corpse up with springs and steel rods. That sudden sitting up when the lid was removed, and the outthrust arm had been neat Wentworth's booming of accusing words without moving his lips had done the trick. In the end, Roscoe Sinclair's corpse had exacted vengeance upon his murderer.

One of the policemen thrust forward, gun half raised.

"But who are you?" he demanded. "How do you know all these things? How do we know that you aren't one of these conspirators, too?"

Wentworth smiled. He stooped over Tony Sinclair's body and lifted it with an easy heave of his shoulders, set it upon the table so that it leaned back against the box. He held it there with his left hand and with his right he drew a cigarette lighter from his pocket. He pressed its base to the forehead of Tony Sinclair and when he had removed it, a blood-red brand was burned there, a vermilion spot with hairy legs, *the seal of the Spider!*

For an instant, the paralysis of fright held them and in that instant Wentworth acted. He pushed the bodies of the two Sinclairs, along with the table and box, crashing to the floor. He hurdled the sprawling heap and was at the window-sill before the policemen, cursing, could jerk up their guns.

Between police and Wentworth, from the coffin of Roscoe Sinclair a spurt and then a torrent of gray tear-gas gushed. Wentworth snatched up a chair, tossed it through the window, and slipped away.

Behind that veil of tear gas, men sneezed and coughed and cried out in torture and fear. Guns blasted harmlessly.

A chemical-saturated handkerchief pressed over his face, Wentworth felt his way swiftly around the wall. The Spider's work was done. The Silver Bill would never pass. The leader of this far-reaching conspiracy was dead and the police would make short work of the Communist army at the gates of the capital. Yes, now at last, the Spider could claim victory. In New York, Nita would be waiting. Together they might snatch some few moments of happiness before once more, the suffering of humanity called Wentworth forth to fight its battles.

Wentworth eased out the door of the cloakroom, smiled back at the turmoil behind him, at the stumbling, reeling men who milled in blind circles. He closed the door softly. Distantly a radio squawked.

"Gentlemen," boomed Senator West, "I agree that this Silver conspiracy is infamous, but there is nothing we can do. We, the entire Senate, the people of the nation, are helpless, helpless."

The Spider laughed.

www.ingramcontent.com/pod-product-compliance
Lightning Source LLC
Chambersburg PA
CBHW020439180626
46812CB00003B/1307